DECEPTION

KATHLEEN HELMS

ZZYYZX PUBLISHING

This book is a work of fiction. Any reference to historical events, people, or real places are used fictitiously. Other names, characters, or events are products of the author's imagination, and any resemblance to actual events or persons, living ir dead, is entirely coincidental.

Deception / Kathleen Helms - 1st ed

Library of Congress Control Number: 2021914923

Ebook ISBN 978-1-7361836-2-5

Paperback ISBN 978-1-7361836-1-8

For Madison Cooper
The art of conversation is not lost on you my friend

PROLOGUE

Taos, New Mexico

The first time the old man had felt eyes on him had been in the grocery store three days ago. He had been placing a box of cereal in his cart when he had felt the familiar prickle at the base of his neck. He had straightened and looked around, but seen no one. The next time he felt the prickle had been yesterday as he was walking in the woods around his house. The hairs on the back of his neck had risen as he walked along the trail. He had scanned the woods and, again, seen nothing. The third time he felt eyes on him had been this morning. He had stepped out onto his front porch intending to cross the yard and get fire wood from the shed. Immediately he had felt the sensation of someone watching him. He had stepped back into his house and locked the door. Now, with daylight fading and his stack of firewood in need of replenishment, he stepped cautiously onto his front porch. He lifted the canvas sling he used to carry firewood and walked carefully to the shed, his footsteps crunching in the newly fallen snow. He opened the door and stepped inside. The fading light did little to illuminate the dark corners of the small building. He quickly filled the sling with firewood and walked back to his house. He entered and closed the door with an audible sigh.

He stacked the wood by the fireplace and added a few logs to the flames. It was cold in the mountains above Taos, New Mexico. He poured himself a glass of whiskey and settled into the chair in front of the fire. He took a sip and felt the liquid fire travel down his throat and settle in his belly. He felt tears prick at his eyes and blinked them back. He supposed there was no shame in an old man crying, but pride kept the drops at bay. He felt a deep stab of regret. Because of his own weakness he had lost everything. Memories, like wisps of smoke, floated in his mind. He found that if he focused too hard on them they simply disappeared. His wife, his child, his grandchild, and his great grandchild, all lost to him forever.

The creak of his bedroom door opening brought him out of his reverie. He turned slowly. His mouth dropped open when he saw the man standing there, but no sound came out. The searcher had found him. His forty-six years of hiding in plain sight were over, as was his life.

1

LOYAL TRUESDALE

Loyal sat on his couch in his new home on Los Robles street in Carlsbad, California. A tiny black kitten perched on his left shoulder. It was the day after Thanksgiving and he was thinking about all he had to be thankful for. There was a lot. He closed his eyes and mentally returned to the Saturday in July when everything had begun. In his mind's eye he could see himself sitting in his buggy in the parking lot of the Lake Wohlford Cafe. In his hand he held a digital wallet, a form of payment from a woman he had helped. The first thing he had done when he had seen the wallet was call his friend and attorney, Maynard Lily. Despite it being a weekend day, Maynard had agreed to meet Loyal at his law office. They had plugged the wallet into Maynard's computer and used the encryption code provided to access the amount the wallet held. The wallet was small, but the amount was large. Very large. Knowing it was more than he could handle, Maynard had passed Loyal off to Antoinette Horvath, the legal firm's resident expert on all things tax related. Loyal had met with Ms. Horvath the following Monday. The cryptocurrency had been listed as income, a healthy amount had been set aside for taxes, and the rest had belonged to Loyal. When all was said and done, he had walked away with nearly $900,000.000.

Loyal reached up and rubbed the top of the little cat's head. It purred and snuggled in closer to Loyal's neck. The first thing Loyal had done was start a bank account for his, at that time, unborn grandchild. The child had since been born. Stella, Mitch, and little Mason had spent Thanksgiving Day with Loyal. Since becoming pregnant and giving birth Stella had developed what she called an "interest" and Loyal internally called an "obsession" with her ancestors. Loyal had broken a long silence and told her everything he knew about her mother, Michelle. Stella had known Loyal's mother, Rita, all her life and had few questions about the woman. She and Mitch had named their newborn son Mason in a nod to Rita as Mason was her maiden name. Stella's latest interest was Loyal's father, Walker. Loyal had not seen or heard from his father since he was eleven and was not eager to discuss the man. He and Stella were still dancing around the subject.

The second thing Loyal had done was gift $50,000.00 to Pat O'Keefe, former co-worker and good friend. When Pat and his wife, Olive, had seen the size of the check they had tried to refuse it. Loyal had insisted they take it and suggested they consider putting it toward the purchase of their first home. While Loyal intended it to be a gift, he and Pat both knew it was also an apology of sorts. In the end they had accepted the check.

. . .

The third thing Loyal had done was purchase the house he was sitting in at the moment. He had moved in on Thursday, October 31st; Halloween Day. Once his friends who had helped him move were gone, he had gone in the small garage to organize his tools. In the quiet of the garage he first heard the meow. Loyal had set some sandwich meat on a paper plate and stood in the shadows. In moments a tiny black kitten had emerged, crossed the room, and started eating hungrily. It had taken Loyal four days, and five packages of sandwich meat, to make friends with the little guy. Loyal had walked to each of his neighbor's houses with a picture of the cat. Nobody claimed it. Loyal named him Boo, since he was found on Halloween. By the Tuesday after he found Boo, Loyal had installed a cat door in the door between his kitchen and the garage. Food, a litter box, a complex cat post, and a small cat bed had been purchased, and Boo and Loyal were both officially moved in.

2

WALKER TRUESDALE - DECEMBER 1958

Walker Truesdale was out of his element. He had reluctantly agreed to accompany his younger brother, Jameson, to a Christmas dance at University of Washington. Jameson was five years younger than Walker and their personalities could not have been more different. Jameson was handsome in a flashy way, very outgoing, and quite the ladies man. Walker was handsome in an understated way, quiet, and reserved. As he surveyed the bright decorations, dancing couples, and laughing groups of attendees Walker regretted agreeing to come. He was considering leaving when he saw her. She was all the way across the large hall. Her back had been turned to him, but she swiveled to say something to a person passing by her group and he saw her face. Walker made his way across the hall and approached her group. He placed his hand on her arm to get her attention. She turned and their eyes met. That was all it took.

The next six months passed in a blur. Walker spent every free minute with Rita. His job as an engineer with Boeing, working on the newly formed 727 project, kept him busy from 8:00-5:00 Monday through Friday. Rita was a senior at UW and was kept busy during the weekdays as well. Weekends and evenings were their time together. Walker took Rita to dinner and the movies, but the majority of their time together was spent taking long walks and talking. As the young couple grew closer, Rita made it abundantly clear that when she graduated in June she would be returning to her hometown of Fallbrook, California. Her father was suffering from lung cancer and likely did not have long to live. Rita was an only child and felt a responsibility to return to Fallbrook so that her mother would not be alone. As the month of June grew ever nearer Walker realized that he did not want to live without Rita in his life. He proposed, she accepted, and after her graduation Walker went with her to Fallbrook.

3

PATRICK O'KEEFE

Pat slid the step stool a few feet to the left and climbed its three steps. He reached up and pulled the last of the painting tape down, then descended the steps and looked around the room with a satisfied smile. He and Olive had moved their family into their new home in early October. They had found it necessary to look a bit inland for a house they could afford and had ended up in San Marcos. They had found a four bedroom fixer-upper in a rural area of the city. The room Pat had just finished painting was his infant daughter's room. Ava had been born just days before escrow closed and was still sleeping in a bassinet in Pat and Olive's room.

Pat balled the tape up in his hand, lifted the step ladder and walked out of the room. He tossed the tape in the trash and returned the ladder to the garage. He walked to the dining room and looked out the sliding glass doors. Olive was pushing Sullivan and Piper on the swing set Pat had recently installed. She wore Ava in a sling across her chest. Pat still found it hard to believe they owned their own home. The unexpected gift from Loyal, combined with about half of their savings, had made it all possible. They were actually paying less per month for their mortgage than they had been for rent on their small condo in Carlsbad. His commute to the Sheriff's Department was longer but well worth it.

The thought about his commute brought Pat's mind back to a case he was currently working on. It had been just two days ago that Len Hammond, a homicide detective that Pat seriously disliked, had leaned into his office.

"Got a minute O'Keefe?" he had said.

Pat had closed his computer and nodded. Hammond had entered and sat down.

"I'm working the fire on Socorro Lane. Husband made it out the upstairs window, wife is deceased."

"Yeah," Pat had said, "I heard about that."

"Something is off with the husband," Hammond had said. "You have time to look at him?"

O'Keefe had nodded and said, "Send me the file."

Hammond had left Pat's office and less than thirty minutes later the file had arrived in his inbox.

Frederick and Colleen Young had been asleep in their house on Socorro Lane when fire broke out. Frederick had jumped out the second story window, Colleen had not escaped. In his notes Hammond had indicated that something felt off about the husband's story. Obviously they could not get the wife's point of view. O'Keefe, who's specialty was computer forensics, planned to start digging on Monday.

4

ANTONIO SHAW

Tony sat at a window seat of the BearClaw Bakery and Cafe in Taos. The remains of his breakfast, a BearClaw special consisting of two eggs, rosemary potatoes, and homemade bread, sat in front of him. He signaled the waitress for another cup of coffee, sat back, and and thought about the events of the past week. Tony had such extraordinary luck that many of his friends and family referred to him as Lucky Tony. True to form, he had recently been lucky yet again.

Tony didn't remember his first bit of unbelievable luck. He had been just three months old at the time, but he knew the story well. His grandfather had made sure of that. Tony's mother, Francesca, had been born when her parents were in their forties. They had despaired of ever having children and had been overjoyed by her arrival. They had doted on their only child and spoiled her terribly. When she had become pregnant at eighteen years old her father had insisted on marriage. It was an unhappy union. When Francesca had shown up on her parent's doorstep with a black eye and split lip her father had sent her young husband packing. The husband had more injuries when he left than he had inflicted on his young wife. The marriage was annulled and Francesca and infant Tony moved in with her parents.

One day Francesca went into the bathroom with her young son. She locked the door, drew a bath and slid into the water. She lay young Tony on her chest and slit her wrists. Sometime later Tony's cries attracted his grandfather's attention. The man broke down the door and found his daughter and grandson in a bath of blood red water. By some miracle Francesca had remained upright. Tony's body was submerged in the cold water, but his face remained above it. His grandparents had adopted him and raised him with far more rules that they had imposed upon their daughter. Tony grew into a respectful, handsome, intelligent, athletic, and lucky young man. He graduated high school, attended UCLA, and earned a degree in business. Upon graduating college he joined his grandfather's business. Now twenty-seven years old, he was well liked and respected by his grandfather's business partners, friends, and their sons.

It was luck that had brought him to Taos. A friend had called and offered him the Airbnb and the ski lift passes. He had flown to Albuquerque a week ago and spent his days on the slopes above Taos. On his second day he had stopped at the local grocery store to pick up some supplies. It was there that he had seen the old man. The picture his grandfather had shown him so many times was from nearly fifty years ago, but

Tony had been sure this was the man his grandfather had spent half a century looking for. He had watched from behind an end cap of Progresso soup as the man placed a box of cereal in his cart. Seeming to sense his eyes the old man had paused and looked around. Tony had stayed behind the wall of soup. He had watched as the old man purchased his groceries and then had followed him into the parking lot. He had memorized the license plate on the old man's truck, raised his phone to his ear, and placed a call.

5

LOYAL TRUESDALE

Loyal woke early, fed Boo, then went for a jog along the beach. The skies were a dark gray, the wind was gusting, and the ocean was a mass of dark roiling water. The air smelled like rain. Loyal jogged about half a mile then turned and retraced his steps. The sprinkles started when he was about a block from his house. It began raining in earnest just as he reached his front door. Loyal showered and dressed in faded jeans and a gray sweatshirt. Just as he was settling on the couch with a cup of coffee his phone rang. He stood quickly and coffee sloshed out of the mug and onto his pants. He swore under his breath but hurried to the phone. He looked at the caller ID, hoping for Trinity. It was Maynard Lily, longtime friend and occasional lawyer. Not Trinity, but still high on Loyal's list of desired phone calls.

"Hey Maynard,"Loyal said.

"You have some time this morning?" asked Maynard. His normally booming voice sounded washed out and tired.

"You okay?" asked Loyal.

"I need to ask a favor of you," said Maynard.

"Of course," said Loyal, "anything you need."

"I'm at home," said Maynard. "Can you come over? I'd rather talk to you in person."

"I'll leave now," said Loyal.

"Thanks man," said Maynard. He hung up before Loyal could say anything else.

Loyal blotted the coffee off his jeans then slipped on some socks and a pair of tennis shoes. He shrugged himself into a jacket, gave Boo one last pat on the head, and headed out to his truck. When he had received his unexpected windfall Loyal had traded his well used Altima in for a gunmetal grey Nissan Titan. He slid into the truck, backed out of the driveway, and headed toward Rancho Santa Fe. Maynard lived, along with his wife Lucinda and daughter Anastasia, on Rambla de las Flores. The long drive curved up a slight hill. Tall stately eucalyptus trees lined the drive. They twisted and swayed in the wind and rain. The drive opened up at the top of the hill onto a huge flagstone circular driveway. The sight of Maynard's home never failed to take Loyal's breath away. A four car garage sat to Loyal's right. The massive seven bedroom, nine bath house sat to his left. It was a single story in some parts, a two story in others, and looked like it had been plucked up from Italy and flown to the United States. Loyal parked and, head bent against the torrent coming from the sky, hurried to the front door. He rang the bell and moments later Lucinda opened the door. As always, Loyal was struck by her beauty. She stood about an inch taller than he did. Her skin was the color of a warm mocha latte and her eyes were an unusual shade of dark brown with specks of honey mixed in. She smiled and waved Loyal in. He shrugged out of his coat and hung it on a rack in the foyer. "Shoes too, please," said Lucinda with a warm smile. Loyal removed his tennis shoes, then turned and gave Lucinda a hug. "He's in the den," said Lucinda.

"Thanks," said Loyal. He made his way through the house to the den. The heavy wooden door was closed so he knocked once then opened it and stepped in.

The room was dark with the exception of a roaring fire in the large stone fireplace. Maynard stood in front of it with his back to the door. He turned as Loyal entered and crossed the room to greet him. Loyal was taken aback by the sight of his friend. At just over 6' 3", Maynard usually commanded a room. Today he was stooped and his coal black skin was tinted with an ashy tone.

"Thanks for coming," he said. Like his complexion, his normally booming voice was faded.

"Maynard," said Loyal, "what's up?"

"I've got a situation, Loyal," he said. "This time I need your help." Maynard walked to the bar and poured himself a small glass of whiskey. "You want a drink?" he asked. Loyal shook his head. "It's a little early for me. What is going on Maynard?"

Maynard took a sip of the whiskey and waved his hand in the direction of two brown leather chairs positioned in front of the fire. The two men walked silently to the chairs and sat. Maynard leaned forward and placed his elbows on his knees. He swirled the amber liquid in his glass. Loyal remained quiet. After nearly a full minute of silence, Maynard began to speak.

6

LOYAL TRUESDALE

"I made a reckless investment, Loyal," Maynard said. He kept his head down, his eyes focused on the whiskey as he swirled it around in the glass. "It is a big land deal developing a large commercial property in San Diego. There were six investors, including myself, and the guy who set the whole thing up; Damien Sallwell." He looked up and met Loyal's eyes. "I had my PI, Arnie Crenshaw, check the guy out. He came up clean." Maynard looked down again. "I set the account up. He should never have been able to access the money, but he did. He disappeared with it four days ago."

"How much were each of you in for?" asked Loyal.

"Five million each."

Loyal did the mental math. "30 million."

Maynard looked up again, met Loyal's eyes, and gave a small nod. He stood up and walked to his desk. When he turned back he was holding two pieces of paper. "This is the only picture I have of Sallwell." He handed one of the papers to Loyal. It was a picture of a group of five men. Maynard pointed to a bald man in the middle of the group. His back was to the camera, but he had turned and placed his left hand on the shoulder of the man next to him. His profile was visible. "I set Arnie on him as soon as I realized the funds were missing. Arnie became focused on this." He handed Loyal the other paper. It was an enlarged picture of Damien's left hand. It was slightly blurry, but Loyal could easily make out the large ring on his fourth finger. "Arnie thought it looked custom made. He started his search in Albuquerque, New Mexico." Maynard turned to look at Loyal again. "I spoke with Arnie yesterday afternoon, about one o'clock our time. Sallwell was an alias, Loyal. Arnie didn't have the real name yet. He told me he was on his way to Taos to meet with a man who might have information about the ring." Maynard paused again and rubbed his hand across his forehead. "I got a call this morning. Arnie was in a car accident last night. He's in intensive care in Albuquerque."

"What is it you want from me, Maynard?" Loyal asked quietly.

"Would you go out there Loyal?" Maynard asked. "Dig around and see what you can find?"

Loyal was silent for a long moment. "I don't have a PI license, Maynard."

"I know, but you are a damn good detective Loyal." Maynard took a long sip of the whiskey. "I've got five angry investors breathing down my neck. This could break me."

Loyal stood and walked to the window. The wind was forcing the rain sideways and the angry drops were pelting the glass. He watched for a moment then turned back toward Maynard. "Give me everything you have Maynard. Every detail that Arnie gave you, plus all the information regarding the real estate investment. I'll need the names of the other investors as well." Loyal saw Maynard's shoulders slump in relief and he held up a cautioning hand. "I'm not promising anything yet Maynard," he said. "Give me a day to look at everything and think about it."

Maynard nodded. "Thanks Loyal," he said.

Loyal and Maynard spent the better part of two hours discussing the situation. When he left his friend's house Loyal carried a plastic storage tote full of documents related to the investment. He tried to drape his jacket over the tote as he ran through the rain to his truck. He headed North on Interstate 5 and exited at Palomar Airport Road. He drove through the local In-N-Out for a burger and fries, then headed home. He tucked the tote and the bag of food under his jacket to protect it from the unrelenting rain as he ran from his truck to his front door. Once inside he set everything on the counter, removed his wet shoes and jacket, and sat at the kitchen counter to eat and think.

7

WALKER TRUESDALE - JULY 1959

Walker stood at the alter of the First Baptist Church of West Fallbrook. He was dressed in a dark brown suit. His brother Jameson, dressed similarly, stood behind him and slightly to his right. Both men's eyes were focused on the front door of the church. As the first strains of the wedding march echoed out, the door opened and Rita and her father stepped into the church. Walker watched as they made their way down the aisle. Rita's father, Edgar, was so thin and frail. It appeared to Walker that Rita was supporting her father rather than him supporting her. Edgar was close to his last days and had somehow rallied to walk his only child down the aisle. Their steps were slow and measured. The last strains of the wedding march faded away before they reached the alter. Edgar handed Rita's arm to Walker then sat down in the first pew next to his wife.

Reverend Henry Howell, the newly installed leader of the historic church, kept the service short. Walker supposed it was in deference to Edgar who desperately needed to return to his bed. The reception was held at the Mason family home. It was a large farmhouse with a wraparound porch situated on 57 acres. Edgar Mason had spent his life farming the land. His father, Edmond, had planted olive groves among the many oaks that dotted the property. Over the years Edgar had removed many of the olives and replaced them with avocado trees. The avocado groves had flourished under Edgar's care. The small group of reception attendees gathered under the shade of a giant oak in the front yard of the farmhouse. June, Rita's mother, had prepared a lunch of fried chicken with deviled eggs, pasta salad, and a cucumber watermelon salad. Once everyone had eaten their fill the cake was brought out. Walker and Rita sliced it and tenderly fed each other a bite. The party continued until Walker and Rita slid into his pale blue Ford F-100 and headed to the L'auberge in Carmel, California for their honeymoon.

8

LOYAL TRUESDALE

Loyal nibbled on his burger while he read through all the documents. He pinched off tiny bits of the meat and fed them to Boo who was sitting on the barstool next to him. Loyal was not a financial wizard, but everything he read about the investment made sense to him. He read all of Arnie's reports and the notes Maynard had taken while speaking to Arnie by phone. They had spoken less than two hours before Arnie's car accident.

Knowing he probably wouldn't be given any information, Loyal called the hospital in Albuquerque. He was informed that, yes, Arnie Crenshaw was a patient in their hospital, but due to privacy laws no information about his condition could be released to Loyal. Loyal hung up and called Maynard. He answered on the third ring. His voice sounded hollow and his words were slightly slurred.

"How did you find out about Arnie's accident?" Loyal asked.

"My business card was in his wallet and my number was the last one he called," Maynard replied.

"Does he have a wife or kids," Loyal asked, "any family that you know of?"

There was silence on the line for a moment. Loyal was wondering if Maynard had nodded off when he said, "He's divorced. I think he might have a kid or two." Maynard paused then added, "Does this mean you are gonna help me out?"

"Still thinking about it," said Loyal, "I'll get back to you soon."

Loyal texted Pat O'Keefe asking if he had time to meet for lunch. Pat responded quickly saying that today wasn't good for him, but that he had time the following day. Loyal responded, suggesting The Chart House in Cardiff at 12:30. Pat responded with a simple *yes.* Loyal called the restaurant and made reservations. With nothing else on his to-do list, he wandered into the garage and looked at his buggy. One of his buggy friends, Brett, had suggested getting a vintage CB radio for the buggy. Brett had kindly offered to help him install it if he found one. Looking at the buggy's dashboard, Loyal could see that there was plenty of room for a CB. He walked back into the house and settled on the couch. His set his computer in his lap and Boo arranged himself on Loyal's left shoulder. He spent the next several hours searching for period correct CB radios.

9

DEAN HAMILTON

Dean Hamilton, formerly known as Damien Sallwell, sat in an easy chair in front of his massive stone fireplace. He watched the flames flicker, dance, and change color and considered his position. He felt he was in fairly good shape. Hamilton had spent the last eighteen years very quietly stealing money from investors. He usually pulled one job a year, occasionally he managed two. The amounts usually ranged somewhere from $200,000 to $500,000. The job he had pulled on Maynard Lily and friends was his biggest and his last.

Hamilton was a skilled hacker. He never exposed his skills by doing something stupid or showing off. He simply slid silently beneath the surface manipulating and rearranging. Five hours after Lily and associates had deposited their money Hamilton had already rerouted it through multiple banks and accounts. The final deposit, into his bank in Taos, had come from an overseas account and looked like dividends paid to him from overseas investments. Hamilton paid taxes on all his investment dividends and, on paper, was an upstanding citizen.

Hamilton was also very skilled with makeup and changing his appearance. He kept his head shaved and had a variety of wigs and toupees to choose from. The Lily job was the first time he had worked with a shaved head. He had manipulated his eye color with contact lenses and made his nose and cheeks appear bigger and more fleshy with makeup. He glanced one more time at the pictures in his hand. He was always conscious of cameras and tried to avoid them when possible. He had been unaware that Lily had taken this shot. His profile looked nothing like he looked now, it was the ring that was the problem.

Hamilton had received a phone call the previous day from Marci, a jeweler in Santa Fe. She had told him that a private investigator had stopped by the shop with a picture of what she was sure was a ring she had designed for Hamilton. She hadn't recognized the man wearing it.

"I was mugged in Arizona last week," Hamilton had replied. "They got my wallet and the ring. Is the investigator still there?" he had asked. "Can I talk to him?"

"I told him I didn't recognize it," Marci had said. "I wanted to talk to you first. Do you want his name and number?"

Hamilton had answered in the affirmative, activated a burner phone, and called the PI, Arnie Crenshaw.

10

PATRICK O'KEEFE

Pat wasn't sure why Loyal wanted to meet for lunch. He found himself hoping it was just for a friendly meal and not for a favor. He couldn't imagine that Loyal had already gotten himself involved in another situation that would require Pat's connections at the Sheriff's Department. Pat considered Loyal a dear friend, but at the same time was determined not to allow himself to be swept up in another drama involving Truesdale.

Olive approached Pat from behind and slid her arms around his waist. She rested her head on his back and held him for a long moment. Pat spun around so that he was facing her and wrapped his arms around her as well.

"Everything ok?" Olive asked. Her head was against Pat's chest and her words came out soft and slightly muffled.

"Yeah," he said, "I'm going to have lunch with Loyal tomorrow."

Olive leaned her head back and looked up at Pat.

"More adventures?" she asked with a smile on her face so he would know she was just teasing. Pat shook his head with a smile.

"Just lunch," he said.

A small cry from down the hall interrupted their hug. Olive gave Pat one more squeeze then turned and went down the hall to their bedroom where Ava had been sleeping in her bassinet. Pat peeked into the living room. Sullivan and Piper were deeply engrossed in an episode of Peppa Pig. Pat knew Sullivan watched the silly show because Piper liked it. He smiled at the thought that the big brother was already so protective of the little sister. With Olive nursing Ava and the kids watching TV, Pat decided to take a minute to review Hammond's arson case again. He sat down at the kitchen table with his lap top and accessed the files Hammond had sent him.

According to Frederick Young's statement, he and his wife Colleen had been asleep when the fire broke out. He had awakened to the smell of smoke, crawled to the bedroom door, and placed his palm against the wood. The door had been hot, indicating that the fire was just outside the door. He had attempted to awaken Colleen. Apparently she took sleeping pills and he had been unable to rouse her. Colleen's weight had made it impossible for Frederick to lift her, so he had decided his best option was to escape and bring help. He had jumped out of the second story window and miraculously sustained only minor soft tissue injuries. A neighbor had seen the flames and called 911. By the time the firefighters arrived the house was fully engulfed in flames.

. . .

Pat leaned back from the computer, closed his eyes, and let the details float around in his mind for a minute or so. He had learned over the years that if he just let his mind relax the detail he was searching for would somehow rise to the surface. Today the detail that floated to the top was the fact that Frederick had sustained only soft tissue injuries from a jump out of the second story window. Where were the broken bones? Pat opened his eyes and returned to the computer. He Google searched the phrase *what bones would break if someone jumped out a second story window.* He received 2,500,000 results in .61 seconds. He chose the top answer which was from the website Quora. The answer posted was from a firefighter and former paramedic. He explained that the only way to survive such a fall without major or fatal injuries was to do a parachute landing fall, or PLF. A PLF involved landing a specific way on one's feet for a micro second, then crumpling to one side and initiating a complex roll. Pat Googled Frederick Young's image. The man was about 5'9" and lacked muscle tone. His thin legs were topped by a round belly. In the picture he had his arm around a woman of similar height. She also lacked muscle tone, but in a different way than Frederick. Although Frederick was out of shape, despite the belly he was still relatively thin. Colleen Young was not.

Pat accessed Frederick Young's Facebook page. The fact that it was set to private was not a problem for Pat. Soon he was scrolling through pictures posted to the account. Pat spent some time looking and never found one picture that even suggested that Frederick Young had any type of athletic ability.

He and Colleen spent most of their time at fancy restaurants with similarly out of shape friends. The more pictures he saw of Frederick Young, the more Pat came to believe that this man could not have pulled off a PLF. How then had Frederick jumped from a second story window and sustained minimal damage to his body? Hammond was right, Pat thought, to have doubts about Frederick Young's story.

11

ANTONIO SHAW

Tony had friends with all kinds of skills. After memorizing the license plate of the old man he had called one of these friends and requested information about the owner of the truck. It hadn't taken his friend long to text him with the information he desired. Soon he had the man's name and address. When Tony had read the man's name he hadn't been able to hold back a smile. He had called his grandfather immediately. Although his grandfather was old and frail he had insisted on coming to Taos. He had been waiting nearly half a century for this moment and wasn't going to miss it. A private jet to bring his grandfather and his nurse had been chartered. While Tony waited on his grandfather's arrival he had surveilled the old man's mountain home.

His grandfather had arrived the following day. His chartered plane had landed at Taos Regional Airport located just nineteen miles away from the actual town of Taos. Tony had picked up both his grandfather and the nurse. He had been dismayed to see that the old man required oxygen at this elevation. Tony had been aware that his grandfather did not have much time left on this earth and had been thrilled that he was going to be the one to deliver the old man to him. They had spent a quiet night in Tony's airbnb. He had related everything he had learned and he and his grandfather had created a plan. The plan had been executed the following afternoon.

After Tony's grandfather had flown back to his home in Southern California, Tony had decided to stay in Taos a few more days to keep an eye on the situation and see if any new developments arose. Before his grandfather had flown away he had stressed to Tony that if the old man's son should arrive in Taos no harm was to come to him. The issue had been with the old man, not the son. Tony had agreed.

12

WALKER TRUESDALE - SEPTEMBER 1959

Edgar Mason passed away in his sleep on a warm dry night in September. He had been alive but weak when June snuggled in beside him and fell asleep. When she woke he was cold and stiff. Her shriek had brought Walker and Rita out of a deep sleep. They had raced to her bedroom and found June on the floor curled in a ball and keening loudly. Rita had taken control of her mother and Walker had summoned Edgar's doctor and the local sheriff. The funeral was held three days later. Edgar was well known and beloved by the residents of Fallbrook. His service at First Baptist Church of West Fallbrook and burial at Fallbrook Masonic Cemetery were well attended. The women of the church flocked to the Mason's farmhouse with food and drink for the reception. June, dressed in black, held court in the family room. Walker and Rita stayed in the background. Both were devastated by the loss.

The mood in the farmhouse was somber in the weeks following

Edgar's death. Although they had all known it was coming, the reality of Edgar's absence was difficult for the small family. June became a shadow of her former self and spent most of her time in the den. She refused to sleep in the bed where her husband had died. Walker got rid of the old bed and brought in a brand new one. At this point June declared that she could no longer sleep in the bedroom she had shared with her husband. In the end Walker and Rita moved into the master bedroom at the top of the stairs and June moved into the small guest bedroom on the first floor.

Edgar had employed one ranch hand. Walker hired another and left the care of the groves to the two men. He found employment at General Dynamics and the small family settled into a routine. Rita took over care of the house and of her mother. At the end of each day the three of them sat at the table and had dinner together. After dinner was cleared and the kitchen cleaned Rita often read to Walker and June from whatever novel she had checked out of the small Fallbrook library. Walker enjoyed this time immensely. It seemed to him that his love for Rita continued to grow with each passing day. When he held her in his arms at the end of each day he tried to explain the evolution of his feelings. She would hold him tight and say that she felt the same way. Walker prayed that it was true. Without Rita his life would be an empty shell.

13

DEAN HAMILTON

Hamilton had told Crenshaw the same thing he told Marci, that he had been mugged in Arizona and the ring had been stolen. Despite the snow falling heavily outside, he had convinced the PI to come see him in Taos. He had given Crenshaw an address about ten miles west of his own home, a vacation house he had known was unoccupied. He had packed a box of disposable hand warmers, a long rope, a flashlight, a Glare Mout Plus dazzler, and a long handled reacher grabber into his Range Rover and driven to a secluded pull out he knew along the PI's route. The snow had been falling steadily and the road had been deserted. Hamilton had picked this spot specifically because he had known it dead ended at the address he had given Crenshaw and it was unlikely anyone else would be traveling on it. Once parked, he had activated a few hand warmers and waited.

Hamilton had known how long the trip would take Crenshaw and had planned his arrival time to be about twenty minutes before the PI would arrive. When he had seen the approaching headlights through the snow, Hamilton had pulled out the Glare Mout and shined the non-lethal laser directly at the driver. Crenshaw had done just what Hamilton had hoped and slammed on the brakes. This action had put the PI's truck into a skid which ended when the truck had broken through the barrier and tumbled over the side. Hamilton had slipped out of the Range Rover and peered over the edge. The truck had been on its side, headlights still shining, about 20 feet down. Hamilton had tied the rope to a still stable portion of the barrier and, reacher grabber and flashlight in hand, had made his way down to the mangled vehicle.

The truck had tumbled on its way down and landed on the passenger side. The driver's window had been shattered and Hamilton had used his gloved hand to push the remaining shards out of the way. He had barely bothered to look at the PI who's face had been covered with blood. Illuminating the interior of the vehicle with the flashlight, Hamilton had seen what he was looking for by the passenger door. A large manilla envelope had been thrown during the crash, but was still intact. Hamilton had used the reacher grabber to grasp the envelope and had gently maneuvered it past the gravely injured driver and out the window. Once the envelope was out Hamilton had seen the driver's phone. He had tried multiple times to grab it but it had kept falling from the reacher grabber's grasp. Not wanting to be found at the scene should someone pass by, Hamilton had abandoned the phone and used the rope to pull himself back up the incline.

. . .

Hamilton stared at the fire and went over everything again in his mind. He looked again at the pictures he had found in the envelope, then slowly fed them into the fire. He watched as they curled, then disintegrated. Hamilton pulled his lap top back into his lap and looked again at the article from this morning's Taos News. The article was short, simply stating that a snow plow driver had come upon the scene of a single car accident. The driver was in critical condition at a hospital in Albuquerque. His identity was not listed. That fact did not matter to Hamilton, he knew exactly who the injured driver was.

14

LOYAL TRUESDALE

The rain woke Loyal at 7:16 on Sunday morning. He rolled over and went back to sleep. It wasn't until Boo climbed on the bed and stuck his little face right up against Loyal's that he finally slid out of bed. He slipped into sweatpants and sweatshirt and gently picked up Boo from the bed. They walked to the kitchen where Loyal prepared coffee for himself and canned tuna and dry cat food for Boo. Loyal sat at the kitchen counter and sipped the dark warm liquid while Boo sat on the floor beneath him and munched on his breakfast. The day was dark and cold; the rain unrelenting.

Loyal spent the morning puttering around his house. At 11:45 he changed into jeans and flannel shirt, pulled a jacket on, and dashed through the rain to his truck. The drive from his house to The Chart House took about twenty minutes. He parked in the parking lot on the south side of the restaurant and waited in his car until he saw Pat pull into the lot. Pat parked next to Loyal and the two men walked quickly through the downpour to the restaurant's entrance. They were seated right away at a table with a perfect view of the angry ocean outside the glass. The tide was in and the waves crashed on the rocks outside the windows. The glass was speckled with drops from the spray.

The waiter appeared at their table. Loyal and Pat ordered beers then perused the menu. When the waiter returned with their beers both men ordered beer battered fish and chips. They took sips of their beers and leaned back in their chairs.

"Olive is wondering if you are embarking on another adventure," Pat said with a smile.

"Not really," said Loyal, "but I can use a favor. It is an easy one and you can clear it with the Captain first of you want."

Pat leaned forward. "What's up?"

"You remember Arnie Crenshaw?" Loyal asked.

"Sure," said Pat, "the PI from Carlsbad. I've met him a few times."

"He's doing work for Maynard Lily in New Mexico," said Loyal. "He was in a pretty bad car accident yesterday. He's in a hospital in Albuquerque. Maynard wants me to go visit him. The hospital won't let me near him without family consent." Loyal paused and took another sip of his beer. "I know Arnie is divorced and I think he has a kid somewhere. I was wondering of you could locate the kid so I can ask permission to visit Arnie."

Pat smiled. "Sure," he said, "that's an easy one. I'll do it tomorrow."

The waiter reappeared with their fish and chips. He set a plate in front of each man and inquired if they needed anything else.

Loyal and Pat both shook their heads. The two men ate in silence for a minute then Loyal said, "You working on anything interesting?"

Pat finished chewing his bite then said, "As a matter of fact I am. Hammond asked me to do some work on one of his cases." He paused and looked directly in Loyal's eyes. "I have to admit that I'm not thrilled about working with him."

"Hammond is an ass Pat, but he's a good detective. He let personal feelings get in the way on the case last April. Just do the job and put your feelings about him aside."

"Did you hear about the house fire on Socorro Lane?" Pat asked.

"Yeah, I think so," said Loyal. "The husband made it out and the wife is deceased?"

"Yep," said Pat, "Hammond gets a bad vibe from the husband. I haven't met the guy yet, but did some superficial digging and I have to admit I feel the same."

"You have good instincts Pat," said Loyal. "If something is there you will find it."

"Thanks Loyal," said Pat. "Hey," he added, "you want to come over and check out the new house? You haven't seen it yet."

"I'd like to Pat," said Loyal, "but there is somewhere else I need to stop this afternoon. I promise I'll get by there to see it soon."

15

LOYAL TRUESDALE

Loyal exited The Chart House's parking lot and headed East towards Rancho Santa Fe. When he had driven through the small town the previous day he had realized it had been well over a year since he had visited Marco Barrossa. Barrossa lived in Rancho Santa Fe and had sponsored Loyal in motocross races when Loyal had been in his teens and early twenties. Loyal had visited the man periodically over the years. He found himself wondering as he drove if Barrossa was even still alive. If he was he would be well into his eighties.

As he drove Loyal let his mind drift back to the first time he had met Marco. It had been the summer after his father had vanished into thin air. Loyal had been eleven years old and filled with rage. Walker had given Loyal a Yamaha 125 for his eleventh birthday, then disappeared the very next day. Loyal had spent hours each day riding the motorcycle around their property. He had been pestering his mom non-stop about racing at Carlsbad Raceway. On this day she had finally relented. They had loaded the bike into his dad's old Ford and driven to the coast. Walker's abrupt exit from their lives had strained the family budget. Rita had no money for racing gear. Loyal had worn jeans and a sweatshirt.

Loyal had gotten the hole shot in his race and had led the pack on the first lap. It was on the second lap that he had misjudged a small jump and had ended up on the ground with his still running motorcycle beside him. He had lain there a moment, his elation at the possible win transformed into despair. When Loyal had started to rise a middle aged man wearing khakis and a button down shirt had hopped the barrier and helped Loyal pick up the bike. "You got this," he had said. Loyal had finished the race, but had not been able to get back to the front of the pack. When he had parked his motorcycle by his dad's truck his Mom had smiled and said, "good job." Loyal had thrown his helmet in her direction and said, "I crashed. Weren't you even watching?" As he had stomped away he had heard her say, "Yes, but you finished Loyal. You earned some points for the series, that's what's important."

Loyal had walked back to the track and pretended to be watching the next race. He hadn't really been seeing anything. He had just been so angry. A bomb had been building inside him. It had been made up of equal parts rage, sadness, and betrayal.

"Your dad know you talk to your mom like that?" Loyal had recognized the low voice and the East Coast accent. The man who had helped pick up his bike was standing next to him. Loyal had bitten his tongue hard enough to draw blood. He had been certain that if he opened his mouth the bomb inside him would detonate and cause irreversible damage. The man had accepted Loyal's silence. When Loyal had felt he could control himself he had turned and looked at the man.

"My dad's not around," he had said.

The man had held out his hand and said, "Marco Barrossa." Loyal had shaken his hand and said, "Loyal Truesdale."

"You have some raw talent Loyal," Marco had said. "I'm looking for someone to sponsor. What do you say we go talk to your mom?"

Loyal brought himself out of his memories as he pulled up to Marco's gate. A guard, carrying a clipboard, stepped out of a small building on the outside of the fence and approached Loyal's truck. Loyal rolled his window down.

"Loyal Truesdale for Marco Barrossa," Loyal said.

The guard shook his head. "Mr. Barrossa isn't receiving visitors today."

"Will you tell him I stopped by?" Loyal asked.

The guard made a note on the clipboard and nodded then returned to his building. Loyal made a u-turn and headed back toward Carlsbad.

16

ANTONIO SHAW

Tony stayed away from the old man's house for several days after his death. On Sunday afternoon he parked some distance from the house and hiked to it. He approached from the back. There were no official vehicles in the driveway, no crime scene tape, no activity at all. The old man's death had been made to look like a suicide. It appeared the police had believed that scenario. He walked to the shed. Snow had been falling for the past few days. No bloodstains showed on the cold, white blanket. Tony approached the house. With gloved hands he tried the front door and found it locked. The mud room door on the side of the house was locked as well. Tony didn't need to get into the house again anyway. He had searched it thoroughly before killing the old man. There was nothing in there that could lead back to his grandfather.

As he turned to hike back to his vehicle, Tony heard the sound of an approaching engine. He slipped behind a stand of trees and watched as a newer model Subaru, it looked like the

Forester from his vantage point, pulled up to the house. The driver, a short plump woman with long gray hair, slid out of the car. She mounted the front steps, inserted a key into the front door, and entered the house. This was unexpected. Tony was aware that the old man had one son. Who, then, was this woman and what was her relationship to the old man?

Tony remained behind the stand of trees for over half an hour. The woman remained in the house. Snow had started falling again and, despite the fact that he was wearing cold weather clothing and footwear, Tony found himself shivering. He briefly considered going in the house and confronting the woman. He was curious about her and wondered if the old man had told her anything about his past. Eventually common sense and numb feet won out. He simply memorized her license plate number and hiked back to his vehicle. Half an hour later he was back in his airbnb warming himself in front of a roaring fire. He had written down the woman's license plate number and would ask his friend for another favor in the morning.

17

WALKER TRUESDALE - AUGUST 1960

While Walker spent his weekdays at General Dynamics, it was the weekends that he most enjoyed. He found that he loved the life of a farmer. He purchased a used Yamaha YA-1 and taught himself to ride. Sometimes he would travel around the acreage alone, sometimes he would have Rita hop on the back and take her with him. On this particular day Rita was on the back. Her left arm was wrapped around his torso, her right held a small picnic basket containing a bottle of wine and some cheese and crackers. Neither rider wore a helmet and Walker smiled when he heard Rita's laughter burbling in his ear. He rode them to their favorite tree. It was a giant avocado tree in a far corner of the property. Walker had never seen one so large. The leaves were plentiful and when Walker and Rita climbed about half way up they were completely hidden from view. They would sit in the tree for hours at a time talking about their dreams and hopes for the future. Sometimes they would bring a blanket and lay beneath the tree, making love in the shade of the giant.

. . .

Today they climbed the tree and sat comfortably in the embrace of its branches. They sipped wine and nibbled on the cheese and crackers. Walker told Rita that his brother, Jameson, had called him at work the previous day and told him that he was going to be in the San Diego area the following week. Walker admitted to Rita that he was worried about Jameson being so far away in Seattle. His younger brother lacked the maturity and common sense that Walker possessed. Rita suggested that Jameson come stay with them for a few days while he was in the area and Walker readily agreed.

Jameson arrived the following week. He roared up the drive in a bright red 1958 Ford Thunderbird convertible. He had the white top down and arrived in a cloud of dust. Walker and Rita stood on the front porch in stunned silence. Jameson slid out of the car and approached the porch at a run. He wore high waisted white pants with a navy blue short sleeve button down shirt tucked into them and a light brown belt securing everything. On his feet he wore, without socks, a pair of navy leather boat shoes. His eyes were shaded by aviator sunglasses. He bounded up the steps and hugged Rita then Walker. Walker returned the hug then looked at his brother in disbelief.

"You look like you are auditioning for a yacht commercial," Walker said. "What's with the outfit? And where did you get that car?"

Jameson removed the sunglasses and squinted at his brother. "I've got a real good gig going on right now," he said. "Finally making some real money." He glanced back at the Thunderbird. "She's a beauty isn't she?" he asked.

"Sure is," said Walker. He motioned towards the door. "Come in and tell us all about it."

18

PATRICK O'KEEFE

Pat arrived at the Sheriff's Department just after 8:00 on Monday morning. True to his word, he began digging into Frederick and Colleen Young's personal lives right away. They had been two months shy of their tenth wedding anniversary when the tragic fire occurred. Both had been excessive users of Facebook and the course of their lives together had been fairly easy for Pat to plot. They posted lots of pictures of themselves on various vacations, eating out with friends, and lounging in the backyard of their coastal home. Privacy issues aside, this was one of the reasons Pat and Olive did not have Facebook accounts. To them it just seemed that most people used Facebook as a way to brag about their seemingly perfect lives. Looking at all the pictures, Pat found himself wondering if Frederick and Colleen ever connected on a more intimate and personal level.

Pat was still deeply bothered by the fact that Frederick had not sustained any injuries from his leap from the second story window. The previous evening Pat had taken the stepladder out into his backyard and tried to master the parachute landing fall. He had not been very successful. What he had learned, however, was that the move took substantial athletic ability. Judging by the images he had seen of Frederick the man was lacking in that department. Pat's one takeaway from studying the images of Frederick was that the man appeared to have an absence of muscle tone.

There was a quick knock at his door and Hammond entered. "You looking into Frederick Young?" he asked.

"Yeah," said Pat, "and I see what you mean. Something is off." Pat paused. "I just don't see how he could have jumped out that window and escaped major injury." Pat took a moment to describe the PLF and his attempts to master it the previous evening. "I'm going to dig deeper today," he said. "As soon as I find something I'll let you know."

Hammond nodded. "Good. I emailed you the video of his interview," he added. "You might want to check that out." Pat nodded and Hammond walked out of the office.

Interacting with Hammond always caused Pat to think about Loyal. In this way he remembered that he was supposed to be looking for Arnie Crenshaw's next of kin. Within five minutes Pat had the address and phone number for Dwight Crenshaw. Arnie's only child lived in Pineville, North Carolina about twenty minutes South of Charlotte. Pat texted the information to Loyal, then opened his email and found the video Hammond had mentioned. Pat leaned back in his chair, put his feet on his desk, and hit play.

19

LOYAL TRUESDALE

Loyal woke early on Monday morning. The clouds were dark and heavy. He burrowed back under the covers and tried to drift back into sleep, but had no success. Eventually he slid out of bed, pulled on his bathrobe, and headed to the kitchen. His first order of business was brewing coffee. His second order of business was feeding Boo. The little cat sat at Loyal's feet while he mixed a can of tuna with some dry cat food. While the cat ate Loyal poured himself a cup of coffee and walked to the living room window. The window was large, taking up the better part of the wall, and one of the things that Loyal loved about his new home. He opened the curtains and looked out. The clouds were nearly black and definitely threatening rain.

Loyal walked back to the dining room table and sat. The pile of papers he had gotten from Maynard was still spread across the surface. Loyal reviewed the timeline once again. Damien Sallwell had first approached Maynard just over a year ago. He had retained Maynard's services in four separate real estate deals before bringing up the deal in San Diego. At this point Maynard trusted Sallwell and only had Arnie do a cursory background check, just deep enough to satisfy the other five investors. Sallwell did not put any of his own money toward the deal. An account had been set up at the Wells Fargo in Rancho Santa Fe. Apparently Sallwell had figured out a way to transfer the funds. Maynard was working with the bank and the local FBI office to try and track the money.

Loyal's phone pinged announcing an incoming text message. He stood and walked to grab it off the kitchen counter when it rang, announcing an incoming call. The caller ID informed Loyal the call was coming from Taos, New Mexico. Normally Loyal would not answer an unknown number, but he thought the call might possibly be related to Arnie Crenshaw, so he answered.

"Hello," he said.

"Hello," said a female voice, "this is Francine Blackwater attorney at law. I'm looking for Mr. Loyal Truesdale."

"This is Loyal."

"Mr. Truesdale I'm very sorry to be the one to inform you of this," said the attorney. "Your father passed away several days ago."

Loyal felt a wave of dizziness crash over him. He felt nauseous and thought for a brief moment that he might throw up. He sat heavily on the barstool beside him. For a moment he was unaware of anything, then he realized he was still holding the phone and that the attorney was still talking. He interrupted her.

"I'm sorry Ms?" he said.

“Francine Blackwater,” the attorney said.

“Yes, I’m sorry Ms. Blackwater,” Loyal said, “I missed some of the content of your conversation. Can you repeat yourself please?”

“I’m sure this is quite a shock for you Mr. Truesdale,” said Blackwater. “I prepared your father’s will over thirty years ago. He left everything to you.

The words “I don’t want anything from him” crowded into Loyal’s mouth. He pressed his lips firmly together to prevent them from escaping. Instead he said, “I haven’t seen or heard from my father since I was eleven Ms. Blackwater. Saying I’m shocked is definitely an understatement.”

“Is there any possibility you can come to Taos?” asked Blackwater. “I’d like to go over the details of your father’s estate in person if we can.”

Loyal was silent for a moment. The enormity of what he was hearing was overwhelming. His father, gone for decades, found but gone again. Dead.

“Are you still there Mr. Truesdale?” asked Blackwater.

“Yes,” answered Loyal, “I’ll check flights and get back to you.”

“You’ll need to land in Albuquerque, Mr. Truesdale,” said Blackwater. “You can arrange a rental and drive to Taos. I’d suggest a four wheel drive. It is snowing here and the forecast is for more. Your father’s home is just outside of town. If you don’t want to stay there I can suggest several Airbnb’s. My office is in downtown Taos.”

“I’ll call you back when I know my itinerary,” said Loyal.

Blackwater thanked him, expressed her sympathy once more, and disconnected.

20

LOYAL TRUESDALE

Loyal sat heavily on the couch and tried to contain his swirling thoughts. All these years his father had been just a few states away. Loyal felt the familiar rage from his childhood return with force and fury. The man he had known for the first eleven years of his life would not have walked away from his family. Loyal had struggled with this thought for years. At age eleven he had been old enough to really know his father. Walker Truesdale had been a man of honor and high moral standing. Young Loyal had held out hope for his return for nearly a month. When that hope evaporated rage filled the void left behind.

Sitting on his couch now, Loyal thought back to the first time his anger at his father had exploded out of him. Rita had been in the kitchen preparing dinner. Walking through the living room, Loyal's eye had been caught by a picture on the fireplace mantle. The picture had been taken on a camping trip the previous summer. Loyal and Walker stood side by side. Walker's arm was slung casually over Loyal's shoulders and both were wearing big goofy grins. Just the sight of the picture had sent a surge of adrenaline through Loyal. He had snatched it off the mantle and flung it against the stone fireplace. The loud crash had brought Rita running from the kitchen.

"Why aren't you mad at him?" Loyal had screamed at her. "Why don't you hate him? Why do you keep fucking pictures of him on our mantle?" Loyal had pushed past his mother and out the door. He had climbed on his motorcycle and ridden out to the far edges of the property. The sun had set by the time he had returned. Rita had left him a foil covered plate of food and gone into her bedroom. The shattered frame remained where it had fallen. Loyal had cleaned the mess and thrown everything in the trash. He had eaten his dinner and apologized to his mother. Hours later Loyal had crept through the silent house and plucked the picture from the trash. He had placed it between the pages of a book his father had given him; My Super Book of Motorcycles and Motorbikes.

Loyal stood and walked to the small bookshelf against the wall of the living room. He lifted the red paperback and couldn't help but smile. The color illustrations were so 1970's. This was the only book Loyal had kept from his childhood. Although he had not opened it since that long ago night Loyal knew exactly where the picture would be. He let the pages fall open and held the picture up to the light. It was perfectly preserved. Loyal had tried to prepare himself for the emotions that would surely flood his system at the sight of the picture. Surprisingly, he simply felt numb.

. . .

Loyal tucked the picture back in the book and replaced it on the bookshelf. He opened his laptop and found a flight departing from Ontario airport for Albuquerque at 7:00 the following morning. He booked the non-stop flight then rented a 2018 GMC Sierra 1500 with five driver selectable operation modes, snow/wet being one of the options. He calculated that the flight, car rental, and drive to Taos would take about five hours. When he called Francine Blackwater back he was directed to voicemail. He left a message with his flight details and his approximate arrival time in Taos. Before he hung up he added that he would be staying at Walker's house.

After disconnecting Loyal saw the small icon that indicated an unread text message. He remembered the text that had arrived just before the phone call. He opened it now and saw that it was from Pat and contained contact information for Dwight Crenshaw. Loyal called Dwight, who had no interest in visiting his father in New Mexico, but was happy to give Loyal permission in exchange for an update after the visit. Loyal then placed a call to Maynard which went to voicemail. He informed his friend that he would visit Arnie in New Mexico but that he wasn't making any promises about looking for Damien Sallwell. After he disconnected from Maynard's voicemail Loyal directed his thoughts toward the two women in his life.

He decided to reach out to Trinity first. He sent a text asking if she had time to talk. Her one word reply arrived quickly; *tonight.* Trinity was an agent with the Office of Strategic Investigations. She was based out of Quantico but was rarely there. Her work involved nearly constant travel. Loyal was aware that she was working on uncovering spying operations within the five Chinese consulates on American soil. He was not privy to classified details and had no idea where Trinity actually was at the moment. His next call was to his daughter, Stella. Although Loyal tried to keep the emotion out of his voice when she answered, Stella knew immediately that something was wrong.

"Are you okay Dad?" she asked.

"Yes," said Loyal, "is Mitch with you?"

"Yes."

"You should probably put the phone on speaker," said Loyal. "I have news that you will both want to hear."

Stella put the phone on speaker and Loyal gave them the few details he knew about Walker's death. Stella had lots of questions and Loyal realized as she asked them that he had no answers.

"It was such shocking news," he said, "that I forgot to ask any questions. I'm flying out tomorrow morning. I'll have more information for you tomorrow night."

"You need a ride to the airport?" asked Mitch.

"No thanks," said Loyal, "I don't have any idea about when I will be returning. I'll leave my truck in long term parking." He paused, then added, "I was wondering if you could feed Boo."

There was a long silence on the line. Loyal could picture Mitch and Stella having some type of nearly silent conversation.

"Why don't we just stay in your guest room?" Mitch finally said. "It would be easier than driving back and forth every day."

Loyal breathed a sigh of relief. "That would be great," he said.

21

ANTONIO SHAW

Tony's friend worked his magic with the New Mexico DMV and soon Tony knew the identity of the woman who he had seen at the old man's house; Francine Blackwater, attorney at law. This made sense. The old man had likely had a will drawn up at some point and she was probably the executor. Her office was in historic Taos. He decided to pay Ms. Blackwater a visit.

Although only twenty-seven years old, Tony was already a very rich man. Not quite as wealthy as his grandfather, but well on his way. Being adopted by his grandparents was another example of Tony's luck. When he had turned eighteen his grandfather had given him information regarding his biological father and asked if Tony wanted to reach out to the man. Tony had declined. His grandfather then offered to legally change Tony's last name to his own. This offer was also declined. Tony kept the name Shaw as a reminder of how things could have been if fate hadn't taken the path that it had. Instead he legally changed his middle name to his grandfather's last name. This had greatly pleased the man. Now, with his grandmother long buried and his grandfather unwell, Tony was poised to take over the entire business.

Tony dressed in the nicest clothing he had brought with him. When he checked his reflection in the mirror he was satisfied that he looked the part; wealthy patron of the arts. He drove to historic Taos and found parking in a paid lot. He walked to Ms. Blackwater's office and stepped inside. A bell tinkled as he entered the tiny office. The woman he had seen the previous day at the old man's house was sitting behind the desk. She stood as he entered.

"Can I help you?" she asked.

Tony smiled sheepishly. "I'm hoping so," he said. "I'm afraid I'm hopelessly lost. I'm looking for the Parson's Gallery but my gps has sent me here."

The attorney smiled. "No worries," she said, "happens all the time. You are close actually. Parson's is just on the other side of Bent Avenue." She pulled a piece of paper from the printer and drew a quick map. "You can walk from here," she said, "then you won't have to worry about finding parking again."

Tony accepted the map from her. "Thank you," he said. "Your office is beautiful," he added, "have you been in this space long?"

"Since 1972," said the attorney, "getting close to retiring actually."

"Not taking new clients?" asked Tony.

"Afraid not," said the attorney. She smiled then added,

"Sadly, it seems like most of my existing clients are passing away."

"That must be hard," said Tony. "Being here that long many of them are probably friends."

She nodded. "One of my best just passed six days ago. Still wrapping my brain around that one."

Tony shook her hand and offered his condolences on the loss of her friend. He thanked her again for the directions and exited her office.

22

PATRICK O'KEEFE

Pat watched the video twice. He hated to admit it, but Hammond handled the interview well. He asked all the important questions multiple times and phrased slightly differently. Frederick Young never missed a beat. His story was consistent and believable, except for the part abut the jump out of the second story window. He claimed his wife, Colleen, had taken her usual sleeping pills around 9:00 and gone to bed about fifteen minutes later. Frederick had followed her to bed around 10:00. Frederick had woken sometime later and smelled smoke. He had crawled to the bedroom door and felt the heat behind it in the hallway. Unable to awaken Colleen he had, in desperation, jumped from their bedroom window and landed on the lawn below. The hit had stunned him and the next thing he remembered was his neighbor pulling him away from the fully engulfed house. Firefighters and paramedics arrived and Frederick had been transported to the hospital. It was there that he had learned of his wife's death.

. . .

When he spoke of Colleen Frederick seemed truly despondent. The second time he played the video Pat closed his eyes when Frederick spoke of his late wife and the pain sounded genuine. If Pat had not had the information about the difficulty of surviving a jump from that height he would have believed Frederick without hesitation. The fact that Hammond felt something was off spoke to the skills Loyal had mentioned. Pat thought about Colleen Young, fast asleep in her bed as flames and smoke surrounded her. He hoped she had died from smoke inhalation before the flames found her flesh. He found his thoughts kept returning to the deceased woman and decided to begin his forensic investigation by concentrating on her rather than her husband.

Pat was amazed by people's willingness to carry what was basically a tracker around with them all day. Cellular phones were an undeniable convenience. Pat glanced at both his personal and work phones sitting on his desk. But phones left a trail. With a simple court order, which was easy to get because Colleen Young was deceased, Pat was able to access her call history as well as her location history. It was in this way that he learned that Colleen had spent each Tuesday and Thursday afternoon, for well over a year, in the office of Cynthia Taft; a licensed personal and family therapist. Pat pulled up Hammond's interview with Frederick Young. He watched until he got to the part he was looking for. He paused the video, went back a few frames, and played it again. Hammond had asked if Colleen had any medical issues or was seeing any doctors. Frederick had said, "She saw her primary doctor for the sleeping pills. She was going to a weight loss clinic after work every Tuesday and Thursday."

"What clinic?" Hammond had asked.

Frederick had shrugged and looked down. "I don't know. She didn't want to talk about it." He had looked back up at Hammond and said, "She was very sensitive about her weight."

Pat leaned back in his seat and thought about this for a moment. He leaned forward and typed out an email to Hammond.

In the interview F. Y. said his wife was attending a weight loss clinic. She was actually seeing a therapist, and had been for over a year. Therapist's name is Cynthia Taft.

Pat included the address and phone number for the doctor. Hammond's terse response came back quickly.

Got it

Pat sighed. "No thanks necessary Hammond," he muttered under his breath. In truth Pat enjoyed his background role in investigations. He found the leads that the detectives either missed or were unable to access. The leg work was left to the detectives.

Pat stood and stretched his arms toward the ceiling. He exited his office and jogged up and down the back stairs a few times.

The time spent sitting behind a computer was the only aspect of his job he disliked. He made a point of getting up and moving every few hours. Pat returned to his desk and, lacking a court order for Frederick's phone, went back to searching Facebook. Frederick had posted a picture on the evening of the fire. He and Colleen were standing on their back deck. It faced West and Pat could see the glimmer of the ocean in the distance behind them. They each held a glass of white wine and were leaning toward each other. Pat could tell by the angle that Frederick was taking the picture.

23

WALKER TRUESDALE - DECEMBER 1960

Between August and October 1960 two events occurred in Walker's life. Both would prove to have a dramatic effect on his future. The first, and by far the most exciting for Walker and Rita, was that Rita announced she was expecting their first child. They had been sitting in their beloved avocado tree drinking minestrone soup from thermoses. Rita had insisted on the soup rather than their usual wine, cheese, and crackers. They had been sitting on separate branches, each with their spine along the trunk of the tree. When she had told him she was pregnant Walker had straightened up so suddenly that he nearly lost his balance and fallen from the tree. To say that he was overjoyed with the news was a complete understatement. Walker did not know what he had done to deserve such happiness. His life had never felt more complete.

The second event was that Jameson relocated from Seattle to Rancho Santa Fe. He was renting a bungalow on the property of one of his boss's friends. He never really told Walker what his job was, but it was obvious that he was raking in the cash. Walker worried that his younger brother was into something risky, or perhaps even dangerous, but Jameson always seemed happy and at ease, so Walker tried to downplay his concern. Jameson showed up most Sundays to have dinner with Walker, Rita, and June. He always roared into the driveway in a cloud of dust and emerged from his Thunderbird in fancy new clothes of the latest styles. Jameson, always the ladies man, flirted shamelessly with June. Walker and Rita didn't mind. June had been elated about the news of the coming grandchild. She was so focused on the upcoming birth that she had come out of her self imposed shell of grief. Watching her laugh with Jameson lifted both Rita and Walker's hearts.

On this particular day, Christmas, Walker had woken early and spent just over an hour riding his motorcycle around the property. When he returned to the house June was up and in the kitchen making breakfast. Rita was still asleep. She was just over six months pregnant and rested when she could. Walker brought firewood into the house and started a fire in the living room fireplace. By the time he woke Rita breakfast was ready and the house was warm and cheery.

Jameson arrived just after one. As always, he sped up the long drive and arrived in a cloud of dust. The Thunderbird's normally empty passenger and rear seats were piled high with brightly wrapped Christmas gifts. The trunk was filled as well. It took Walker and Jameson multiple trips to carry everything into the house. When Walker set down his last stack and looked at the huge pile of gifts in the center of the living room floor he was flabbergasted.

"This is too much Jameson," he said.

"Relax Walker," said Jameson, "it's not every day a man gets to celebrate his family. It just looks like a lot. It isn't that much at all."

By the time all the gifts were opened Walker could see that his brother had spent a small fortune. He bit his tongue and let the family enjoy the day, but he knew that sometime soon he and Jameson were going to have to have a serious talk.

24

PATRICK O'KEEFE

It was nearly five o'clock and Pat was over two years into Frederick and Colleen's Facebook history when he found a picture that caused him to pause. The picture was taken in some type of medical facility. Frederick, looking pale and tired, was sitting up in the bed. He wore one of those unflattering hospital gowns that open in the back. His smile was weak but genuine. It was Colleen that caught Pat's eye. She was sitting in the bed next to Frederick. She had her right arm around her husband's shoulders and was holding her cell phone out with her left hand to take the picture. As Pat had gone back in time on this Facebook search of the Young's lives he had watched the pounds melt off Colleen. She had gone from wearing shapeless blouses and dresses to sporting form fitting jeans and snug tops. She looked so happy in this picture. her bright smile reached her eyes and the joy shining out of them was real and unmistakeable. There was one sentence describing the picture. It read *Pacemaker success....Thank you Dr. Patek!*

. . .

Pat took a screenshot of the picture then went back to the last picture posted by Frederick and took a screenshot of it as well. He closed down Facebook and brought the two pictures up on the computer screen. He positioned them side by side so he could compare them. When the pictures were placed side by side the difference in Colleen Young's appearance over the two year period was shocking. She had gained a lot of weight. Pat guessed around fifty pounds or more. In the earlier picture her happiness was evident, it was practically exploding out of her. In the last post by Frederick she looked awful. Her face was swollen by the added pounds, her smile was forced, her eyes full of stress and sadness. Pat logged back into Facebook and looked at the last picture again. It had been posted the evening of the fire and had the caption *Another beautiful day in paradise.* Pat was skilled enough to look beyond the posting date and find the date the picture was actually taken. To Pat's surprise, the picture had been taken nearly six weeks before the fire.

Pat looked at the upper right hand corner of his computer screen and saw that it was 5:02. He logged out of everything and shut the computer down. He took a paper notepad out of his desk drawer and wrote two things down. The first line read *cause/origin of fire,* the second read *pacemaker?*

Pat stood and gathered his things. He locked the door and walked quickly down the stairs to reception. He saw Fatima, the main receptionist, heading to the front door. He increased his speed and caught up to her just as she was reaching the exit. He held the door open for her and walked with her through the darkening parking lot to their cars.

25

LOYAL TRUESDALE

Loyal woke six minutes before his alarm was scheduled to go off. He silenced it before it could wake Mitch, Stella, and Mason who were all asleep in the guest room. They had arrived the previous evening and brought pizza from Pizza Port. Loyal had been thrilled. He loved his new home and would not trade it for anything, but he sorely missed his apartment's proximity to the popular pizza restaurant. They had brought a six pack of Pizza Port's Swami's IPA as well. Loyal had enjoyed three slices and two cans before begging off and heading to bed. Trinity had called just after 10:00. She could tell immediately that she had woken Loyal and suggested they talk the following day. Her suggestion changed when Loyal gave her the news about his father. They had talked until nearly 11:00. Although he knew he needed the sleep Loyal had been grateful for her call. Her voice and wise words calmed him and he had slept well upon disconnecting. Loyal's alarm had been set for 4:25 and he had woken at 4:19.

. . .

His flight was scheduled for 7:00 am out of Ontario which was about a ninety minute drive this early in the morning. He had chosen Ontario for two reasons. The first was that it was a much smaller airport than San Diego and the TSA lines were much more manageable. Being an honorably retired peace officer, Loyal had the privilege of carrying his firearm, concealed, in all 50 states. He had packed his PM9 into a locked gun case along with the unloaded magazine. His ammo was in a locked ammo case. He carried an HR-218 card in his wallet. This card was proof for law enforcement that Loyal was allowed to transport and carry a concealed firearm. At the counter Loyal requested a TSA lock on his luggage. This sent his luggage to a different x-ray machine than the average traveler's checked bag. The second reason that Loyal preferred Ontario was that it felt like a much safer place to leave his brand new truck in long term parking. Loyal had packed the previous day. He dressed in comfortable traveling clothes; loose dockers and a long sleeve sweater. He brewed some coffee and drank it on the couch with Boo. It was another rainy day which was unusual in Southern California even in winter. The season had arrived early this year and come in strong. He was backing out of his driveway, windshield wipers working hard, by 5:00.

The flight to Albuquerque was bumpy but uneventful. Loyal tried to sleep, but found himself unable to drop off. He had an aisle seat and was able to stretch his legs out a bit. He spent much of the flight with his eyes closed, resting and thinking abut his father. Before he had driven away, Loyal had taken the picture back out of the motorcycle book and laid it on the kitchen counter. He had placed a yellow post-it note next to the picture and written a short note to Stella. It read:

. . .

Until the day he left he was the best Dad a kid could hope for. I'll call you soon. Love you kiddo, Dad

Loyal deplaned and made his way through the airport. It was larger than Ontario and had a very Southwestern feel. He picked up his checked bag from the baggage carousel and then followed the signs that directed him to the car rental shuttle. A shuttle was idling at the curb and Loyal stepped on. There were about a dozen people on the small bus. All were looking at their phones and no one glanced up as Loyal entered and sat. Seeing all those phones reminded Loyal that his was still on airplane mode. He pulled it out of his pocket and swiped the icon that returned it to normal function. The phone dinged immediately indicating a text message. Loyal tapped the icon and saw that he had one message from Stella. It read:

Thank you for the note and the picture Dad. It means more to me than you know. Call when you get settled in Taos. Boo sends his love

Loyal smiled and returned the phone to his pocket. He leaned back and closed his eyes. He was tired already and the journey had barely begun. The car rental offices were just under ten miles from the airport. During the ride Loyal sat, eyes closed, and thought about Trinity. Talking to her last night had been both a relief and a burden. Loyal was not an emotive kind of guy. Talking about feelings and emotions, especially sad ones, was low on his list of favorite things to do. Still, he was grateful for their conversation. Trinity meant a lot to Loyal.

26

PATRICK O'KEEFE

Pat was in his office, computer open in front of him, but his mind was elsewhere. He had woken from a deep sleep early in the morning. His dreams had been distressing, and when he had woken he had turned to wrap his arms around Olive but she had not been in the bed. Heart racing, Pat had jumped out of bed and checked the bathroom. Olive had not been there either. He had peeked in the bassinet and seen that Ava was also missing. When he had rounded the corner into the living room he had found them. Olive, illuminated by the early morning light coming in through the sliding glass doors, had been sitting on the couch holding a sleeping Ava.

"You ok?" Olive had asked him.

"I am now," Pat had said as he sat down beside her. "Bad dreams."

"You were moving around a lot in your sleep," Olive had said.

Not wanting to relive the dream or put the horrific images

in Olive's mind, Pat had simply hugged his wife then headed off to take a shower.

Now, staring unseeingly at the computer screen in front of him, Pat allowed the images to flow through his mind. In the dream he had been in the back yard setting up the play structure. The wind came suddenly and powerfully, thrashing the branches in the trees and blowing the structure over on its side. With the wind came the smell of smoke. Pat turned and saw a wall of orange and red just outside the perimeter of their fence. The heat from the flames singed his skin and his nostrils were assaulted by the acrid smell of burning debris. Pat had spun quickly and run back to his house. He could see Olive and the kids through the sliding glass doors. They huddled together in the living room. The glass from the doors reflected the flames approaching behind Pat and it looked to him as if his family was on fire. In the dream Pat had been unable to open the sliding glass doors. He had rushed around the house, trying every possible entrance, to no avail. He couldn't get in and his family couldn't get out. Just as his home, and family, went up in flames, Pat had woken.

Pat pushed the images away and refocused on the computer. He had sent an email to Hammond inquiring about the cause of the fire and whether an autopsy had been performed on Colleen Young. When Pat had passed Hammond's office on his way in this morning he had seen that Hammond was not in. He wasn't expecting an answer soon. That left him with the other note he had written on the pad of paper before leaving the previous evening. The word *pacemaker.*

27

LOYAL TRUESDALE

The woman at the car rental counter was what Loyal's mom would have called "a hoot". Charlene couldn't have been a day under 75 or a pound over 100. She had bleached blonde hair piled up on top of her head in a messy bun, and bright blue eyes that, when magnified by the glasses she wore, seemed impossibly large. Her smile was bright and white. Despite his somber mood Loyal flirted with her and they had a few laughs. She gave him the keys for his rental and sent him out the side door to the parking lot where another employee would unite him with his truck.

The GMC Sierra was just what Loyal had asked for. The exterior was a muted silver and the interior was black. Loyal slid in and took a minute to adjust the seat to his frame and the rear and side mirrors to his height. He took his PM9, magazine, and ammo out of his bag and loaded the firearm. He slipped the belly band around his waist and slid the gun into it. Feeling complete with his gun back on his waist, Loyal turned on the ignition and spent another minute or so familiarizing himself with the truck's controls and navigation system. When he felt ready to drive he plugged the hospital's address into the navigation system and began following the computerized voice's directions. The drive was easy. He spent less than three minutes on Interstate 25 then exited at Coal Avenue. He followed the navigational directions and found parking in a paid lot on the south side. He entered the hospital lobby and approached reception. He explained to the woman seated behind the desk, she could have passed for Charlene's sister, that he was there to see Arnie Crenshaw and had received permission from the man's son to see him. The receptionist, Betty, spent a moment tapping keys on her computer then looked up at Loyal. "You are all set to see him," she said. "ICU is on the 7th floor." She pointed down the hallway. "The elevators are down that hall. Give your name to the receptionist in ICU."

When the elevator door pinged and the doors opened a flood of people emerged. Loyal entered the empty car and rode to the 7th floor alone. He explained who he was and why he was there to Seth, the man at reception, and was allowed in to see Arnie. Loyal was not prepared for what he saw. Seth explained that Arnie had been in a very bad car accident. His worst injury had been bleeding in the brain. Seth explained that the doctor had removed a bone flap from Arnie's cranium and had induced a coma for two days to allow the swelling to subside. The bone flap had since been replaced and Arnie had been brought out of the coma. Unfortunately, Arnie remained largely unresponsive. The procedure now was to let time pass and see if he improved. Loyal got the sense that Seth was not anticipating that improvement.

. . .

Seth informed Loyal that he was allowed a ten minute visit then left the room. Loyal sat down in the chair next to Arnie's bed. He had met Arnie on a few occasions when Maynard had brought the man to their weekly Tuesday nights at Pizza Port. Loyal looked at the man in the bed. His skull was wrapped and there was severe bruising on the right side of his face. His nose looked broken. An IV snaked its way into Arnie's right arm, and he was hooked up to a variety of monitors that emitted beeps periodically. Loyal tried to pull up a mental image of the Arnie from Pizza Port to compare to the Arnie who lay in the bed before him. As he thought about this and played mental images of the man through his mind Loyal realized that Arnie had the perfect face and physique for private investigations. He was just about as average as a man could be without fading into the wallpaper. He was average height and had average features. There was simply nothing memorable about the guy. If his broken nose didn't heal properly that could pose a problem for Arnie. He'd have a distinguishing feature.

Seth returned in ten minutes and informed Loyal that his visitation was over. As they walked out of the room Loyal asked Seth if Arnie had ever regained consciousness or spoken about the accident.

"Yeah, he's come out of it a few times," said Seth. "The only thing he's ever said is "bright light". Not sure what that means." He paused a moment then added, "Maybe he had a near death experience." Loyal thanked Seth for his time. As an afterthought he turned back and asked Seth if he knew of any good Mexican restaurants in Santa Fe. Seth laughed. "Yeah, of course," he said, "there are tons. Try Maria's on Cordova Road. It's really good food." Loyal thanked Seth again and left the hospital. When he reached his rental truck he took a minute to call Dwight Crenshaw. The call went to voicemail and Loyal left a brief message about his visit to Arnie. He invited Dwight to call back with any questions but doubted that the man would. The world was filled with divorced parents and angry kids. Loyal belonged to the former category but, thankfully, not the latter. He and Stella were about as close as two people could be.

28

PATRICK O'KEEFE

Pat's father, Michael O'Keefe, suffered from a condition called sleep apnea. Sleep apnea, as its name suggests, occurs when an individual is asleep. They basically stop breathing for short periods of time. Michael used a continuous positive airway pressure, or CPAP machine to keep his airways open. What Pat was thinking about now was that his father had told him that the CPAP machine his doctor had prescribed used a cellphone wireless link to connect to the internet and transmit Michael's information to a secure server. His doctor could log on and check Michael's information at any time. Pat was wondering if pacemakers might follow a similar protocol.

Just as he was leaning forward to begin researching this there was a short rap on his office door. He looked up to see Len Hammond entering the office.

"I just spent some time with Colleen Young's therapist," he said as he entered and sat down opposite O'Keefe. "Cynthia

Taft is a nice lady. She didn't want to share any information with me, patient confidentiality and all."

"As her personal representative Frederick can access those records," Pat interjected.

Hammond smiled. "Yes, except Frederick doesn't know about the therapist," he said, "and I have no intention of telling him." Hammond paused. "Ms. Taft did give me one piece of information. When I said that I had my suspicions regarding Frederick she informed me that Colleen was planning on asking for a divorce."

"That's interesting," said Pat. "I noticed that they were just shy of their ten year anniversary when I was going through their Facebook pages."

"Yep," said Hammond, "everyone knows the ten year rule and that after ten years alimony can be awarded. They both worked for an advertising firm in San Diego, but Frederick was the bigger wage earner." Hammond paused as if for dramatic effect. "With that information I have what I've been looking for; motive."

Hammond left the office and Pat sat back in his chair and turned this new information over in his mind. Hammond was right, the fact that she was planning on asking for a divorce did change things. He leaned forward, placed his fingers on his keyboard, and began to research pacemakers.

By three o'clock Pat had a basic understanding of pacemakers. The implanted pacemaker mimics the action of the body's natural electrical system. Some pacemakers are implanted temporarily, some are implanted permanently. Pacemakers, like Pat's father's CPAP machine, can be checked remotely. The pacemaker sends and receives information to and from the doctor's office. This information includes heart rate and rhythm, how well the pacemaker is functioning, and its remaining battery life. Additionally, newer pacemakers have sensors that can detect body motion and breathing rate. These sensors are intended to signal the pace maker to increase heart rate during exercise or strenuous activity.

As Pat was leaning back in his chair to contemplate the implications of everything he had just learned, his email pinged. He opened it and found an email from Hammond.

Autopsy revealed an upper airway free of soot and carbon monoxide was detected in the postmortem blood at 39%. She was alive when the fire started.

Origin of fire is an outlet outside of the master bedroom door. The hallway there is large and has a built in counter. A computer was plugged in and charging there.

29

LOYAL TRUESDALE

When Loyal entered Maria's on Cordova Road into the navigation system he was informed that the trip would take him approximately 56 minutes. He eased back onto Interstate 25. Traffic was light. Loyal set the speed control for 70 mph and soon had left Albuquerque behind him. Bare land stretched out on either side of the Interstate. Every so often a dark green bush appeared in the distance. Loyal passed by several casinos with overflowing parking lots, but saw little else on the drive. He exited the Interstate in Santa Fe and followed the electronic voice's directions until he arrived at Maria's.

At first Loyal thought the restaurant was closed. There was scaffolding assembled around the building and it looked to be in some state of disrepair. Still, he parked and walked around the building toward the back. There he found a door and entered. It may have looked shabby from the outside, but Maria's was fabulous on the inside. He was greeted by the hostess as he walked in. She led him through a series of dining rooms, then down a long hallway and into the bar. Loyal was seated at a table for two. Menus were already on the small table. He was surprised to find an entire menu just for margaritas. Apparently Maria's was famous for the drink and offered over 100 varieties. Loyal considered ordering one but decided against it. He was meeting with the lawyer in just a few short hours and didn't want to show up smelling of booze.

When the waiter arrived with chips and salsa Loyal was ready with his order for beef fajitas and water. He munched on a few chips while he thought about Arnie, damaged and suffering, in the hospital bed in Albuquerque. He wondered what the man could have possibly meant about the bright light. Loyal seriously doubted it had been a religious experience. The food arrived quickly and was delicious. Loyal was surprised by how hungry he was and realized that he had not eaten since the previous evening. When the waiter suggested sopapillas for desert Loyal agreed even though he did not know what sopapillas were. It turned out that soapillas were fluffy fried bits of dough, crisp on the outside and chewy on the inside. They were served with honey drizzled over them. In spite of the fact that he had consumed every bite of the fajitas, Loyal ate all the sopapillas as well. He was just putting the last bite into his mouth when his phone rang.

30

TRINITY GLASS

After her long talk with Loyal Trinity had lain awake in her hotel room in Houston, Texas and found sleep elusive. He had tried to play it off, but Trinity had heard the pain and emotion in his voice. Trinity had tried to push the death of Loyal's father to a far corner of her mind so that she could concentrate on the situation that had brought her to Houston in the first place. She had tried, and she had failed.

It was noon now, and the team of agents that she was working with was breaking for lunch. Her boss, Doug Caldwell, held up a hand as she was walking toward the door.

"Glass," he said, "a minute please."

Trinity stopped and walked back to where he stood. He waited until all the other agents had left the room then asked her, "Where are you today? Your focus sure as hell isn't here."

Trinity looked down, then back up at Caldwell.

"I've got a personal situation Doug," she said. "I could use a few days."

Caldwell held her gaze for what felt like hours but was probably less than one minute. Finally he said, "72 hours Glass. Not one minute more. Be back in this office by noon on Friday." He turned and walked out of the room before she had a chance to respond.

Trinity walked back to the hotel and took the elevator to the fourth floor. She used the electronic key to enter the hotel room that had been her home for the past three weeks and likely would continue to be for the foreseeable future. She sat heavily on the bed, slid her low pumps off her feet, and called Loyal. He answered on the third ring and sounded like he had food in his mouth.

"Is this a bad time?" she asked. She heard him swallow.

"No," he said, "there's never a bad time for a call from you."

"I have 72 hours Loyal," she said. "I can be in New Mexico this evening if you want me there."

"Yes, please," said Loyal. "You'll need to fly into Albuquerque. Want me to pick you up?"

"No," said Trinity, "I'll get a rental. I'll text you when I have my flight details."

"Thanks Trinity," said Loyal. The relief in his voice was audible.

"I'll see you soon," she said and disconnected.

Trinity opened her laptop and booked a flight from Houston to Albuquerque leaving at 3:15. The flight time was two hours and fifteen minutes. With the one hour time difference between the two cities, Trinity's flight would touch down at approximately 4:30 Albuquerque time. She checked the weather in Taos and saw that snow was predicted for the next several days. Trinity accessed the car rental website and looked for something that could handle the snowy roads. She decided on a 2019 full size Chevy Tahoe. It was bigger than she really needed, but she liked the look of it. That done, she packed a bag and ordered an Uber to take her to the William P. Hobby Airport.

31

DEAN HAMILTON

Everything Dean Hamilton owned was custom designed. His home was perhaps the most unique. He had purchased the land, just over seven acres located Southeast of the actual town, after his second job. He had purchased an airstream and lived in it for three years while he planned the design of his future home. During those three years he had pulled off four more jobs and had nearly three million legal dollars sitting in various bank accounts. He lived frugally during those years, always worried that he would get caught. His confidence grew with each successful job and five years in to his "career" he decided to build the house he had been designing. He hired a local architect, Emily Strong, and together they drew up the plans. Hamilton had studied the seasons, the winds, the angle of the snowfall and the way the drifts piled up. He knew the land and its personality as well as any backwoods mountain man.

The house had taken six additional years to plan and build.

From the outside it looked like a large barn. The inside was much more lavish. Each detail was designed to suit Hamilton's preferences. There was a hidden staircase, built into the mountain, that led to a wine cellar far beneath the earth. This is where Hamilton was now. He wandered through his vast collection of bottles and finally decided on a $3,000.000 bottle of Screaming Eagle cabernet. He made his way back through the staircase and into his living room. Through the massive window that dominated the western facing wall of the room he could see that the sky was dark and the snow was falling heavily outside the glass obscuring any view of the trees and hills. Hamilton uncorked the wine, poured himself a generous glass, and sat down in his favorite chair which faced the fireplace. He sat and sipped and watched the flames. He closed his eyes and listened to the crackling sound the flames produced. He thought about fire and how much power and energy it could produce. It was man's folly to think he could control it.

Hamilton opened his eyes and thought about things he could control. The first being safeguarding his future. He had a motto; *It isn't stealing if they give it to you.* He had based his entire adult life around these words. He was not about to give any of his hard earned money back to anyone. He had chosen Taos as his home because the town had unique qualities. It was remote but still offered all the amenities he required. The art scene was thriving and Hamilton was a frequent customer at art and jewelry stores in both Taos and Santa Fe. He was well known for dropping large amounts of money on paintings and jewelry. It was this connection to jewelers and collectors that had saved him from the prying eyes of Arnie Crenshaw.

32

LOYAL TRUESDALE

Loyal was about forty-five minutes outside Taos when the snowflakes began to fall. They were light and fluffy until the elevation began to rise at which point they were falling like a white blanket. At the moment Loyal was driving along the Rio Grande. He could tell there was a steep wall to his right but wasn't able to distinguish if it was made of rock or soil. To his left the Rio Grande coursed through it's channel. It looked to Loyal as if the water was flowing heavily and creating whitecaps on the waves but he couldn't be sure. The heavily falling snow had severely reduced visibility. Loyal pulled over when he saw the opportunity and switched the truck into snow/wet mode. He felt the difference when he pulled back onto the road. He found himself hoping that the weather would clear before he left Taos. He supposed the view of the Rio Grande would be spectacular on a clear day.

Loyal entered Taos about ten minutes before 3:00. He passed by a Baskin Robbins on his right and then saw Hinds and Hinds storage on his left. He was stopped briefly by a red light, then entered the historical downtown district of Taos. Loyal found parking in a paid lot. Francine Blackwater had informed Loyal that he would need plenty of quarters to pay for parking. He had a ziplock full of them in the truck. The cold air slammed into Loyal when he slid out of the heated cab. He reached into the back seat and pulled his jacket out of his luggage. He realized as soon as he slipped it on that the jacket was not nearly warm enough for the weather in Taos. If his stay required more than a day or so he would probably have to purchase something heavier.

Each quarter bought Loyal fifteen minutes of parking time. He began feeding coins into the meter, intending to insert twelve in all. He wore no gloves and his fingers became slightly less nimble as each successive coin dropped into the meter. He dropped the twelfth coin and looked at it laying in the white snow by his feet. Rather than pick up the cold coin, Loyal simply fished another one out of the ziplock and inserted it clumsily. Leaving the snowy quarter for someone else, he turned and made his way to the attorney's office. She had explained that her office was in a tiny alcove opposite an art gallery and a jewelry store. Loyal found the door and turned the knob. A small bell tinkled as he walked in.

Loyal paused as he entered the office. He peeked back outside to make sure he had the correct address, which he did. The office looked more like an art gallery than a law office. There was an oak L shaped desk to Loyal's right. The desk top was empty with the exception of several clay figurines and a beautifully painted ceramic pot. A painting was hung on the wall behind the desk. Loyal had to study it for a moment to understand what it depicted. It didn't actually show the drummer, rather the scene was from the drummer's point of view. Loyal saw the drum and the drumsticks. Beyond that were the dancers. Some were native people wearing brightly colored clothing. Interspersed among the natives were gray ghosts who were dancing as well. Two leather visitor's chairs faced the L shaped desk. To Loyal's left were a gorgeous leather couch and a coffee table made of a wood Loyal did not recognize. It had what appeared to be real turquoise inlays. Loyal moved closer to study it.

"Mesquite," said a voice which caused Loyal to jump. "Harder than oak and maple. Actually ranked up there with teak and mahogany."

Loyal turned and saw a woman standing behind the L shaped desk. He saw now that there was a door behind the desk and slightly to its left. A woman had stepped through it and was looking at Loyal now. She was small in stature, not more than 5'3" but Loyal guessed her weight to be around 150. She had long straight gray hair that was pulled back into a ponytail. Her eyes were such a dark shade of brown they almost appeared to be black. Her cheekbones were sharp, her smile bright and white. "Loyal Truesdale?" she inquired as she stepped toward him with her hand extended. Loyal crossed the small room and held out his hand as well.

"Yes," he said as they shook, "and you are Ms. Blackwater?" She nodded.

"Why don't you can hang your coat on the rack," she indicated a rack just inside the entrance, "and join me at the desk."

Loyal shrugged out of his jacket and hung it on the rack she had indicated then chose one of the chairs facing her desk and sat.

33

TRINITY GLASS

Trinity's plane was wheels up by 3:20. She had a window seat and watched as Houston shrank below her. With a small sigh she closed the window shade and reclined her seat. She closed her eyes and thought about Caldwell's face as he had spoken to her earlier in the day. Trinity could only remember two other times when she had asked for extra time off. Both had to do with Loyal Truesdale. Her job was important to her and she had done it well for many years in spite of various romantic entanglements. What was it about Loyal, she wondered, that inspired her to request time off.

Several days previously Trinity had been in line in a grocery store in Houston when she had heard a snippet from a country song that was playing on the loudspeakers. She wasn't sure of the artist, but the lyric had said *she's got whatever it is, it blows me away.* This was exactly how Trinity felt about Loyal. He had *it.* They had first met the previous April when their cases had intersected. The attraction had been instant and undeniable. Their professional paths had crossed again just last July. While Trinity respected and admired Loyal in a professional aspect, it was their down time together that she truly treasured. Whenever she had consecutive days off Trinity flew to Loyal.

Trinity sat with her eyes closed and thought about her favorite moments with Loyal. She loved long lazy mornings in bed and walks down the beach talking and getting to know each other. They had toured Stone Brewery in Escondido and then spent the better part of the afternoon sipping beer and eating tasty treats. On her last trip to visit Loyal he had driven her out to the desert town of Borrego Springs to show her the giant sculptures that populated the valley. On impulse, Loyal had stopped by the house of his friend Maggie's godfather, Peter. Peter had welcomed them with open arms. It had been late September and the temperature had been in the high eighties. Peter had made cocktails and the three of them had sat by his pool and talked. Afternoon flowed into evening and Peter invited them to stay the night. The three of them had worked side by side in Peter's huge kitchen preparing a meal of spaghetti and meatballs, a large green salad, and crisp garlic bread. They had eaten at an outside table as the sun was setting.

Borrego Springs is a dark skies community, dedicated to the preservation of the night sky. Trinity had never been to Borrego before this trip and as the sun set and the stars emerged she found her gaze continually drawn skyward. Peter noticed this and invited them to his upstairs office where a large telescope dominated the corner of the room. Peter produced a few bottles of wine and the three of them spent several hours sipping and stargazing. Thinking about it now, Trinity couldn't help but smile. The next morning had been spectacular as well. They had woken before sunrise, piled into Peter's jeep, and driven to a spot called Font's Point. Once there, Peter had produced three large travel mugs filled with Irish coffee. They had sat in the sand, sipped, and watched the sunrise.

Trinity had no living family members. Her parents and brother had died years ago. Her parents had been only children, therefore Trinity had no aunts, uncles, or cousins. She was, essentially, alone. Being with Loyal felt right and true. Being with Loyal felt, to Trinity, like coming home.

34

LOYAL TRUESDALE

Francine Blackwater spent several minutes appraising Loyal with those dark brown eyes. He sat quietly, leaning back in his chair with his hands loosely on his thighs, and endured her inspection. At last she gave a slight nod as if answering some internal question and leaned forward, her elbows on the desk and her hands clasped in front of her.

"You look like him you know," she said at last.

"If I remember correctly he was a bit taller and a lot leaner," Loyal said.

Francine smiled and nodded. "Yet there is something about you," she said, "the set of your eyes, the lines around your mouth, the way you carry yourself."

When Loyal had decided to come to Taos he had been determined to make the visit to the lawyer a quick stop. He had had no intention of walking down memory lane with Francine Blackwater. Now though, he found that he was interested. He made a decision to let the conversation play out and see where it led him.

. . .

Francine leaned back in her chair, her posture mimicking Loyal's.

Loyal," she said then paused and added, "can I call you Loyal?"

He nodded. "You call me Francine," she said, "no need to stand on formality among friends. And Dale was one of my dearest."

"Dale?" asked Loyal.

"I'd like to tell you the story of how I met your father," Francine said. "Is that all right? We can get to the legal mumbo jumbo soon enough."

"Yes," said Loyal, "I'd like to hear your story." Surprisingly, Loyal realized that he was speaking the truth.

"It was in June of 1972," said Francine. "I had just opened this very office and had gone to Santa Fe to reward myself with some jewelry from my favorite designer. I was on my way back to Taos when I saw your dad hitchhiking on the side of the road in Española. I drove right past of course, no young woman in her right mind would pick up a man from the side of the road. The thing was, our eyes met as I passed him." Francine paused at the memory. "He looked so damn sad Loyal," she said. "I couldn't shake the image. I went about ten miles then turned around and went back. Sure enough, there he was. Walking along the side of the road looking like he had lost his best friend." She looked Loyal directly in the eyes. "It turns out he had," she said.

"We talked on the drive to Taos. He didn't reveal much about himself except his name, Dale Walker," she looked expectantly at Loyal but he said nothing, "and the fact that he had nowhere to go." Francine leaned forward again, her eyes locked on Loyal's. "We became friends. I helped him get a social security number. Things were different back then, pre Internet. I helped him get a job taking care of rental properties for a man I knew and he stayed on my couch until he saved up enough to rent a small place. Eventually he got his real estate license. That worked well for him. He made enough to buy some land and build his house," she paused then said, "your house now."

"Did he ever tell you his his story?" Loyal asked.

Francine shook her head. "Not really. One time after a few too many whiskeys he told me he had had the love of the best woman in the world and lost it." Francine let that sink in for a moment then added, "He never dated Loyal. I'm assuming it was your mom he loved, and he never stopped."

35

DEAN HAMILTON

Despite the snow falling heavily outside Hamilton felt the need to get out. He decided to head into the historical section of Taos for a drink. There was a bar there called The Treehouse that he frequented. It was located above a restaurant called Lambert's of Taos, stocked high end wines, and the food was decent. Mostly Hamilton just needed to get out of his house. Having already enjoyed one glass of wine, he drove carefully on the newly plowed roads and found parking in a paid lot not far from the bar. His feet made a crunching sound as he walked through the ice and snow to the entrance. Once inside he shed his heavy coat and gloves and made his way upstairs to the bar.

Hamilton lived alone and worked alone. He enjoyed the company of women; the expensive high end sort. His wine cellar was extensive, his fridge stocked up. He did not need to go out to have an excellent glass of wine and a decent meal. He certainly wasn't looking for a one night stand. Still, with no job prospects to research and no disguises or personas to create he felt a bit lost. The bar was not crowded, but as he found a spot and sat, he felt the warmth of being among other humans wash over him. It was a strange sensation to Hamilton, being among people who he was neither trying to deceive or cheat. He found he enjoyed it on rare occasions.

Hamilton ordered the jumbo lump crab cakes and and a glass of Caymus Cabernet. As he sipped and nibbled his mind went back to the PI, Arnie Crenshaw. It was unfortunate that the man had survived the crash. The chance of a snowplow being on that remote stretch of road at that time of day was astronomical. The man was gravely injured however, so Hamilton held out hope that perhaps he would succumb to his injuries. He spent just under an hour in the bar. As he was leaving he decided to pay a visit to his friend Onawa Shanley who owned a jewelry store just around the corner. He couldn't wear his favorite ring anymore and thought perhaps today was a good day to look for something new.

36

LOYAL TRUESDALE

Loyal didn't say anything for several minutes. Thoughts, images, and memories were bouncing back and forth in his brain. Everything was jumbled and he found it difficult to focus on just one thing. Eventually the thoughts, images, and memories untangled and he found he was ready to speak.

"His name was Walker Truesdale," he said.

"Yes," said Francine, "I learned that when I drew up his will."

"You never researched him?" Loyal asked.

Francine shook her head. "It would have felt like a betrayal." She paused then added, " I was tempted, but, no, I never did."

Francine reached down and opened a desk drawer. When her hand reappeared she held some papers. "Dale's will," she said and slid the papers toward Loyal. The will was short and simple and did not take Loyal long to read. Walker had left everything to his only son, Loyal. If Loyal had predeceased Walker then everything was to go to his granddaughter, Stella Truesdale. This stipulation stunned Loyal. His father had known about Stella. The familiar anger flooded Loyal's system once again. Walker had taken the time to track Loyal's life but had never bothered to reach out, not even once.

"You are angry," said Francine.

"Damn right I am," said Loyal. "He left when I was eleven. He devastated our family. I never knew why or where he went. I never knew if he was even alive. Now I find out he was following my life and knew of the birth of my daughter."

"You have every right to feel anger," said Francine. "All I can say is that Dale's love for you and your mother was a powerful force in his life. It never wavered. Again, he never revealed to me the reason that he left, but I can only guess that it had to do with protection."

Francine took the papers back from Loyal and slid them back into the drawer. She stood and said, "Let's get you to the house before we lose all daylight." Loyal stood, shrugged himself back into the coat and followed her to the door.

The snow was still falling when they emerged from Francine's office. Loyal paused to fasten his coat and, sensing movement across the courtyard, peered through the falling snow. What he saw took his breath away. A man, his back toward Loyal, was walking across the courtyard. He looked just like the man who called himself Damien Sallwell. The build and the bald head were identical. As if sensing Loyal's eyes on him the man stopped then slowly turned. As soon as his face was revealed Loyal realized this man was not the same man who was pictured in Maynard's photo. Their eyes met for a brief moment then each man turned away. Loyal looked back after a few steps and saw that the bald man was entering a jewelry shop called Tigua Treasures. Just as he was slipping through the door into the shop the bald man turned and looked at Loyal again. Their eyes met, the door closed, and he was gone.

37

ANTONIO SHAW

Tony had driven to the same spot not far from the old man's house and hiked in again. There was no activity. The more he thought about it, the more convinced he became that if the old man's son was going to arrive in Taos it would likely be this day. He drove back to the historic district and parked in paid parking near Francine Blackwater's office. He inserted enough quarters to last several hours and settled down to wait. He didn't have to wait long. After less than five minutes the attorney rounded the corner. A man followed her. His resemblance to the old man was close enough that Tony was convinced this was the son. He started his car and eased out of the parking lot. He drove straight to his usual spot near the old man's house, hiked in, and waited.

Less than ten minutes passed before the attorney's Subaru and a Chevy truck pulled up the long drive. The attorney and the man from the parking lot exited their vehicles and entered the house. Tony, having learned from the last time, activated some disposable hand warmers and kept his gloved hands in his pockets. His feet were sheathed in newly purchased wool socks and waterproof hiking boots. He watched until the attorney left, then hiked back to his vehicle. It appeared the old man's son was going to stay.

38

TRINITY GLASS

The plane touched down safely in Albuquerque but the landing was rough. The pilot had prepared the passengers. About fifteen minutes before the descent and touchdown he had spoken over the loudspeaker explaining that the winds were strong and the landing would be bumpy. His prediction had been correct and Trinity stepped off the plane with a sigh of relief. She went to baggage and collected her suitcase then followed the signs until she found the shuttle that would carry her to the car rental offices. She stepped on and found a seat near the front. She used the drive time to call Loyal. He answered on the fourth ring.

"Trinity," he said.

"I'm in Albuquerque," Trinity said. "I'm on the shuttle to the car rental offices."

"I hope you reserved something that works well in the snow," said Loyal. "It's pretty thick up here."

"Full size Tahoe," said Trinity. "How's everything going?"

"I just met with the lawyer," said Loyal. "I'm following her out to my dad's place. It is a bit outside of the actual town. I think it would be best if I met you in town and you followed me out."

"That works," said Trinity.

"The drive is going to take you about two and a half hours," said Loyal. "Have you eaten?"

"I'll eat when I get there," said Trinity.

"Put the Taos Albertsons in your navigational system," said Loyal. "I'll make sure I'm there by 7:30. I'm in a silver GMC Sierra 1500."

"Copy," said Trinity. "See you there."

"Thanks Trinity," said Loyal. "See you there."

They disconnected just as the shuttle arrived at the car rental offices. Trinity said a quick thank you to the driver and hopped out. The offices were quiet at this time of day. It was nearing 5 pm and stormy weather was predicted. The clerk was a young man. He was quiet and professional and Trinity was united with her Tahoe in less than fifteen minutes. Thinking about Loyal's query regarding food, Trinity mapped local take out places and decided on Chick-fil-A which was located just off Interstate 25. In less than ten minutes she was ordering a chicken sandwich and a coffee for the road. Trinity ate the sandwich quickly and stuffed the trash in the map pocket. She sipped the coffee slowly. She didn't want to stop again.

39

WALKER TRUESDALE - APRIL 1965

Loyal turned four years old on April 7, 1965. Walker and Rita held a party for their young son. They invited some friends and cooked burgers on a grill in their yard. Walker had installed a giant swing set and the kids played while the adults cooked food, sipped iced tea, and chatted. The sun was bright in the cloudless springtime sky and the mood was festive. The only thing missing was Jameson. Walker had reminded his brother multiple times of the date and time of Loyal's party and Jameson had assured him he would be there. Yet here it was, over an hour after the start time, and there was no sign of Loyal's uncle.

Walker held off as long as he could, but eventually the food was served, the candles were blown out, and the presents were opened. It was just as Walker, Rita, and Loyal were waving goodbye to their last guests that Jameson roared down the drive in his usual dust raising fashion. He brought the Thunderbird to an abrupt halt right in front of Walker, Rita, and Loyal.

When the dust settled Walker could see that Jameson had brought a woman with him as well. The convertible top was down and Jameson and the woman were laughing loudly.

Jameson slid out of the car and went around to help his passenger out. She stumbled as she slid out of the car, grabbed on to Jamesons shirt, and, giggling loudly, righted herself. At this point Walker and Rita could smell the whiskey. Rita gave Walker a pointed look, then took Loyal by the hand and went into the house.

"Hey," Jameson said loudly, "don't take the birthday boy away."

"You missed the party Jameson," Walker said in a low voice.

Jameson attempted to push past Walker. Walker placed his hand on Jameson's chest and stopped his forward progress.

"You need to leave," he said, "go home and sober up."

"No way Walker," slurred Jameson, "me and the little lady brought the party with us." Jameson turned to his date and grabbed her hand. "Come on honey," he said and attempted to lead her past Walker.

"No," said Walker, more forcefully this time. He took the woman by the arm and turned her back toward the Thunderbird. Jameson dropped her hand and took a swing at Walker. Walker blocked the punch, pushed Jameson away, and helped the woman into the car. He closed the door and turned to find Jameson advancing on him. Before Walker had a chance to respond, Jameson launched himself into his older brother and both men tumbled to the ground. Walker hit the dirt hard and Jameson landed on top of him. Walker's wind, and his last bit of self control, were both knocked out by the fall. He pushed Jameson off, rolled to his right and ended up on top of his brother. The first punch hit the side of Jameson's head. The second punch connected directly with Jameson's nose and resulted in a rush of blood. Walker pushed off Jameson and stood. He looked at his brother for a long moment. Jameson was on the ground, writhing in pain and mumbling something unintelligible. Eventually Walker simply turned and walked away.

40

PATRICK O'KEEFE

Pat left the Sheriff's Department at 4:30. His mood was somber with sprinkles of disillusionment mixed in. When he had decided on a career in law enforcement Pat had envisioned himself as a crusader of sorts. He was the guy who was solidly on the right side of the law. His mission, as he saw it, was to right all the wrongs in society and make the world, or at least his small part of it, safe. He had seen things in a very one dimensional way; good versus evil, right versus wrong. Now, nearly ten years in, he saw his naivety for what it had been. In his years on the force, especially the time spent in vice, his innocence had slowly been eroded away. He saw now that the world was three dimensional and filled with shades of gray.

As he drove towards San Marcos thoughts about Colleen Young kept popping into Pat's head. Her therapist's admission that Colleen had been planning on asking Frederick for a divorce was telling. It certainly backed up Pat's impression, based on the dramatic change in her appearance, that Colleen had been unhappy during the last several years of her marriage. Frederick had to have been aware of it as well. Was the possibility of having to pay alimony enough to push someone to murder?

Pat was driving East on Mission Road when he passed a local dive bar called the Cow Shed. He had never been inside but had heard the joke from friends that it should have been named the cow shit. Impulsively Pat pulled over and parked. He hesitated before exiting his vehicle. A high percentage of peace officers were divorced. This was not a club Pat was eager to join. Still, one beer couldn't hurt. He had left work half an hour early so he could drink one and still make it home in time for dinner.

The bar was fairly empty at 5:00 pm on a Tuesday. A few men, they looked like regulars to Pat, were scattered around the bar. Two were playing pool. Pat approached the bar and sat. Although the bar had few customers and there were two bartenders it took several minutes for one of them to approach Pat and ask what he wanted. The woman appeared to be in her late forties. Her stringy hair was pulled back in a severe ponytail. Her eyes were flat and no smile played upon her thin lips. Pat ordered an IPA and drank it quickly. When the bartender asked if he wanted another the word 'yes" slipped unbidden out of his lips. He drank the second one a bit more slowly. It seemed to Pat that the bottles were emptying so fast. When he ordered his third beer he ordered a plate of nachos as well. If Olive was going to be upset with him, he decided, he might at least make it worth his while.

41

LOYAL TRUESDALE

Early evening had arrived by the time Loyal and Francine pulled up to his father's house. There was enough ambient light for Loyal to see that the house was a single story mountain cabin. The snow was still falling as he and Francine exited their vehicles and walked to the front door.

"Dale has a truck with a plow attachment," Francine said as they walked up the stairs to the front porch. "If the snow keeps falling at this rate you might need to use it to get out of here tomorrow."

As Francine inserted the key into the front door and began to turn it Loyal said, "Francine," in a quiet voice. She turned and looked over her right shoulder, her right hand still on the key in the door.

She looked up at him and Loyal asked the question he had been holding back since their phone conversation the previous day. "How did my dad die?" Francine let go of the key and turned so that she was facing Loyal. She grasped his forearms with her hands

"The official determination is suicide," she said. "Single gunshot to his head out by the shed." Even in the dim light Loyal could see that her eyes had filled with tears.

"Do you believe that?" Loyal asked.

"I don't know what to believe, Loyal," Francine said. "The man I knew would never have done that." She paused then added, "Maybe I didn't know him as well as I thought."

"Or maybe his past finally caught up with him," Loyal said. "Where is his body?"

"His will stated cremation," Francine said. "His ashes should be ready to pick up in a few days."

Francine turned back to the door, finished unlocking it, and opened it so that they could step inside. She flicked a light switch on the wall and the inside of the cabin was illuminated for Loyal. Francine crossed the living room to the large stone fireplace opposite the front door and began lighting a fire. Loyal stood just inside the front door and looked around. The living room was large. The floors were wood, Loyal thought pale oak, and covered with what looked to be hand woven Native American rugs. A single large leather chair sat in front of the fireplace. The kitchen was to Loyal's left. A granite island separated the cooking and dining spaces. The dining room table was a small rectangle and there were only two chairs. To the right Loyal saw a small bathroom and a closed door that he assumed led to the bedroom. A bookcase, housing some books and clay figurines, stood to the right of the fireplace.

. . .

Loyal shrugged out of his coat and hung it on a rack in the entry way. A heavy coat, he assumed it was his father's, hung on the rack as well. He stepped forward and bent down to look at one of the rugs more closely.

"Zapotec Indian 100% wool rugs," Francine said, "hand woven." Loyal looked up and saw that she had stood and that a fire was growing in the fireplace behind her. "Dale had good taste," she said. The art is all original and from local artists as well. Come on," she said, "I'll show you around."

Francine walked Loyal through the cabin. She showed him the kitchen appliances and a small washer and dryer located in a mudroom accessed through a door just beyond the dining room table. He glanced in the bathroom, then steeled himself and opened the bedroom door. The room was large, with the same wood flooring as the living room, and a thick woven rug placed near the bed. A large window occupied most of one wall. A fireplace was located opposite the bed, which was a king and supported by a frame made of rough hewn pine. Loyal supposed Walker had made the frame himself. There was a dresser to the left of the fireplace and a matching end table next to the bed. Two frames sat on the end table. Loyal walked closer and looked at the pictures they housed. The first was of Walker and Rita. Loyal was familiar with this picture and knew that it had been taken on their honeymoon. Walker and Rita stood side by side, arms around each other. The blue of the Pacific was visible behind them. The wind was blowing their hair in their faces and they were laughing. The second frame held a picture of Loyal. It had been taken on the same camping trip as the picture in Loyal's motorcycle book. Loyal was alone in this shot. The exception being the trout he was holding in his arms. The sun was shining brightly and a laughing Loyal squinted as he smiled at the camera. The memory of that moment came hard and fast, causing Loyal to take a quick, deep breath.

He turned and saw that Francine had stayed in the living room. He exited the bedroom and rejoined her by the fire. They stood side by side, gazing down into the flames, each lost in their own thoughts. Francine broke the silence saying, "There is no central heat. You are going to want to keep fires in both fireplaces whenever you are here. These rocks," she patted the stones around the fireplace, " absorb and radiate the heat. You should be plenty warm." She handed Loyal the key ring. "Here are keys to the house, the shed, and Dale's truck. She paused, then added, "I haven't figured out what the small one on there goes to yet. I'm sure you will find something that needs to be unlocked." Loyal accepted the keys and thanked Francine. She started to walk to the door, then turned and asked, "Does your phone have signal here?" Loyal pulled his phone from his pocket, checked the bars, and nodded. "Good," said Francine. "Dale has a land line, no cell or internet. I'll text you the land line number." She turned to leave then turned back once more. "I almost forgot," she said, "Dale has a storage unit too. About two blocks from the Historical District. Swing by my office in the morning and I'll give you the keys." With that she was out the door and Loyal was alone.

42

LOYAL TRUESDALE

With Francine gone, Loyal began to look through his father's home more carefully. He started with the kitchen and spent some time familiarizing himself with the location of pots, pans, dishes, and silverware. Everything Walker owned was of good quality and made to last. The house had a decidedly masculine feel that Loyal appreciated. The fridge had a few premixed salads that had seen better days and a steak that was past its use by date. The pantry was stocked with canned and dry goods. The living room was fairly bare. There was no television or computer. Loyal did notice a record player in a cabinet to the left of the living room fireplace. Looking at the fireplace reminded him of Francine's suggestion that he keep fires burning in both fireplaces at all times. He returned to the bedroom. A bronze log holder, filled to the top with cut firewood, was positioned next to the bedroom fireplace. Long matches were on the mantle. Loyal got a fire going in the bedroom and returned to the living room. The bookcase held nothing of a personal nature. There were some books about the history of Taos, the Native American art scene, and plants and animals indigenous to the area. The clay figurines depicted a variety of animals. Loyal was able to distinguish a few as a dog, a bear, and a rabbit.

Loyal returned to the bedroom and looked in the dresser drawers which held Walker's neatly folded clothes, sheets, and blankets. Loyal quickly stripped the bed and remade it. He carried the used sheets and blankets to the mud room and set them on top of the washer. He returned to the bedroom and looked in the end table drawer which held a pair of reading glasses and Walker's wedding ring. Loyal recognized it immediately. It was made of titanium, dark gray, and wide. Loyal lifted it slowly out of the drawer and tried to slip it on his own finger. It got tight at the knuckle. Unsure if he would be able to remove it if he forced it past the knuckle, Loyal removed the ring and replaced it in the drawer. With one last glance at the pictures of his parents and his ten year old self, Loyal turned and walked back into the living room.

He walked to the coat rack by the front door and lifted his dad's coat off the hook. It was heavy and well worn. Loyal slipped his right arm into the right sleeve, hesitated a moment, then slipped his left arm in the left sleeve and shrugged the coat on. His father's scent, unchanged in all these years, enveloped him. Just like that Loyal was ten years old again and back on the camping trip in the Sierra's. Loyal's jacket had gotten wet in the lake so Walker had slid his own jacket over his son's shoulders when the sun had gone down. Loyal had felt so safe and warm in his father's jacket on that long ago night.

. . .

With a shake of his head Loyal removed his father's jacket and hung it back on the rack. It was definitely warmer than his own jacket, but the thought of being enveloped in that scent for any measurable period of time was something Loyal did not feel ready for. He glanced at his phone to check the time. It was nearly 7:00. Loyal slipped his own jacket on and stepped back out into the night. He locked the front door and stuck the keyring Francine had given him in his jacket pocket. He crunched through the snow to his truck, started it up, and eased down the snowy drive.

43

TRINITY GLASS

Trinity pulled into the Albertsons parking lot just after 7:30. The lot was nearly empty and she spotted Loyal's rental truck immediately. She pulled her Tahoe up beside him, cut the engine, and slid out. The wind and snow engulfed her as she walked around her vehicle toward Loyal's. He had seen her pull up and was already out of the truck and moving toward her. He pulled her into his arms for a hug and quick kiss.

"Let's grab some supplies and get back to the house," he said.

Trinity nodded in agreement. They locked their vehicles and, hand in hand, walked into the store.

Fifteen minutes later they emerged with two bags of supplies. Loyal had noticed that Walker did not have a microwave, so they had purchased two frozen dinners that could be prepared on the stovetop. They had also picked out one dozen eggs, a bag of potatoes, butter, a case of water bottles, two bottles of red wine, and a six pack of Lagunitas. They loaded the supplies into Trinity's Tahoe then began the drive back to the cabin. Loyal drove slowly and carefully and Trinity had no problem following him. The track from the main road to the cabin was covered with snow and Trinity breathed a sigh of relief when they both were parked safely in the driveway. As they walked up the steps to the porch Trinity said, "That last part was pretty sketchy Loyal. We might not be able to get out of here tomorrow."

"My dad has a truck and a snow plow attachment," said Loyal. "I'll have to figure out how to use it in the morning."

Trinity put the food away in the kitchen while Loyal added wood to both fires. He took five minutes to show her around his father's home. Trinity was impressed.

"Did he build this place himself?" she asked. "Everything looks custom made."

"Yeah," said Loyal, "My dad was an engineer at Boeing and General Dynamics and really good with his hands. I think he did most of the work himself. According to his attorney, Francine, all the furniture, rugs, and art are made by local artisans."

Trinity slid her arms around Loyal and held him tightly.

"How are you holding up?" she asked.

Loyal kissed the top of her head. "Better now," he said, "thanks for coming Trinity."

She looked up at him. "I don't know about you," she said, "but I could sure use a shower."

Loyal smiled. "You go first," he said.

"You know me better than that Loyal. No need to waste water," said Trinity. She took his hand and turned toward the bathroom.

44

LOYAL TRUESDALE

Loyal sat in the large armchair in front of the living room fireplace. Trinity sat sideways in his lap, her long legs hanging over the right arm of the chair. They were warm, full, and relaxed. The first bottle of wine had emptied fairly quickly and the second had just been opened. Loyal's feelings of anger and anxiety had lessened with Trinity's arrival. After they had eaten, he had called Stella and told her everything that had happened thus far. With nothing left to do until the following day, Loyal was finally allowing himself to relax.

"I'm liking the whole no T.V. no Internet way of living," said Trinity. Her head was on his left shoulder and her breath was warm in his ear. "I saw the record player," she added. "Mind if I check out his collection of music?"

Loyal relaxed his embrace. She stood and walked to the record player. It was housed in a dark brown wooden cabinet that stood about waist high. He watched as she opened the lower cabinet and thumbed through the record selection. She stood without removing anything and opened the top section where the turntable was located.

"He's got a record in here, Loyal," Trinity said. "You ok if I play that? It's a guy I've never heard of, John Prine." She turned to look at Loyal. "You ever heard of him?"

Loyal felt his guts clench at the name. "He was my parent's favorite musician. They listened to his first album all the time." Loyal paused then added, "That was over four decades ago. I'm sure he has a lot more albums out now."

"Can I play it?" Trinity asked.

Loyal let out a silent sigh. "Sure," he said, "why not."

Trinity turned on the turntable and placed the needle in the groove. She settled herself back in Loyal's lap as the first notes rang out. The first song was somewhat of a protest song called "Your flag decal won't get you into heaven anymore." Loyal smiled as he listened. He liked John Prine and hadn't heard this song in many years. The second song to play brought sudden tears to Loyal's eyes. He blinked them back, but couldn't stop the memory that came flooding into his brain, one he hadn't thought about in a long time. He let the entire song play. When it ended he asked Trinity if she could please turn it off.

Trinity did as he asked, then returned to his lap.

"You want to talk about it?" she asked gently.

"My parents used to dance to that song," said Loyal. "My mom told me a few years before she died that they tried for a long time to have more kids but she kept having miscarriages. After an ectopic pregnancy the doctor told her it was too dangerous to keep trying." He paused and gave a half laugh. "She told me that she loved to dance, but my dad didn't. After she learned they couldn't have any more kids he started dancing with her. The last time I saw him they were dancing to that song."

Trinity remained quiet and after a few minutes Loyal continued. "It was the night of my eleventh birthday. My dad surprised me with a motorcycle. It was the best day. We rode around the property together until the sun went down. After I went to bed I heard the music playing and got up. I saw them in the living room dancing to that song." Loyal shifted slightly in the chair. "My mom had her head on my dad's chest and her eyes were closed. When he turned toward me I saw his eyes were closed too. He had tears on his cheeks. I had never seen my dad cry, Trinity."

Trinity leaned back from Loyal and met his brown eyes with her blue. "He already knew he was leaving." Loyal nodded, "Looking back at that moment now, I'd have to say yes."

An hour later Loyal and Trinity were in the king size bed. The room was softly lit by the light of the dying fire. Loyal could tell by Trinity's even breathing that she was asleep. He was as tired as he had ever been, but found that he simply could not sleep. The last lines from the John Prine song kept floating through his mind.

Will you still see me tomorrow?"

"No, I got too much to do"
Well, a question ain't really a question
If you know the answer too

And the sky is black and still now
On the hill where the angels sing
Ain't it funny how an old broken bottle
Looks just like a diamond ring
But it's far, far from me

45

PATRICK O'KEEFE

Pat's mouth was sticky and dry. He lay in bed with his eyes closed silently begging the throbbing pain behind his eyes to go away. He finally opened his eyes, looked to his right, and saw that he was alone in the bed. He closed his eyes again and tried to remember what had happened when he had gotten home the previous night. He remembered his spontaneous decision to stop at the bar. He had downed five fast beers and two shots of whiskey while he was there. He thought he might have eaten something too, but couldn't remember what it might have been. He had definitely been too drunk to drive when he had left the bar. If he remembered correctly, an Uber had deposited him at home.

Pat's memories regarding what had transpired upon his return to his home were murky and fragmented. He was able to conjure up the look of surprise and disapproval he had seen on Olive's face when he had stumbled into the kitchen. Had he fallen? He couldn't remember. Pat eased himself out of bed and studied his naked reflection in the closet mirrors. He didn't see any bruising. His face looked haggard and his eyes were puffy, his skin the color of gray paste. With a sigh Pat stepped into the bathroom and started the shower. He took a long one and kept the water as hot as he could stand it. Despite a thorough scrubbing the smell of stale booze still emanated from the pores of his skin.

Pat dried off, wrapped the towel around his waist, and stepped back into the bedroom. Olive was leaning against the wall, arms crossed tightly across her chest. She eyed him warily, her tension palpable. Pat crossed the room toward her, but saw her stiffen, and stopped just short of reaching her.

"I'm sorry," he said.

"You accused me of a lot of things last night Pat," she said. Pat remained silent. He couldn't remember what he had said and had no idea how to diffuse the situation.

"You don't remember do you?" Olive said.

Pat shook his head. She was holding her eyes firmly on his. Pat wanted to look away but didn't. The silence was deafening. Finally Olive spoke.

"I'm not having an affair, Pat. I spend my days with the kids. There's no one else." She paused. "Everyone has tough days and makes mistakes Pat, but if last night was an indication of how things are going to be then we have a serious problem."

Pat took the last steps toward her and opened his arms. With a small sigh Olive slipped into them.

"It won't happen again Olive," he said. "I swear."

She pushed away and looked up at him then leaned in and

kissed his cheek. As she walked out of the room she turned and said, "And tell Loyal if he is going to get you that drunk he can just take you home with him." When he heard those words Pat remembered that he had blamed the incident on Loyal. Part of him wanted to tell Olive the truth, that he had gotten that drunk by himself. Wanting to avoid the disappointment he would surely see in her eyes, Pat opted to keep that nugget of information to himself. Loyal and Olive's paths wouldn't be crossing any time soon. She would never discover that Pat had lied.

46

WALKER TRUESDALE - JULY 1969

Four years passed before Walker saw Jameson again. He had been so angry at his younger brother for showing up late and drunk to Loyal's birthday party that he had resisted reaching out to Jameson. As time went by Walker realized that he didn't miss seeing Jameson as much as he had thought he would. He never reached out and neither did Jameson, that is until a hot day in July when the Thunderbird, looking a little worse for wear, arrived in its usual cloud of dust.

If Walker hadn't known that it was Jameson he doubted he would have recognized his brother. His "I don't have a care in the world" attitude was gone and replaced by slumped shoulders and downcast eyes. The Thunderbird had dents and scratches and was in serious need of a wash. Jameson's normally fashionable clothes were out of date and hung on his too thin frame. Walker stood on the porch and watched in silence as Jameson mounted the stairs and stood before him. Walker felt a curious mix of anger and pity seep into his heart.

"Walker," Jameson said with a nod of his head.

"You finally here to apologize?" Walker said.

"I'm sorry for a lot of things," Jameson said.

"I was just heading out to check on the groves," said Walker. "You want to take a walk with me?"

Jameson let out an audible sigh and nodded.

Walker usually rode his motorcycle to check the property. Walking the entire acreage would take some time, but he supposed that they might need it. Jameson looked beaten down and close to breaking. Walker wasn't entirely sure he actually wanted to hear his brother's tale of woe, but he supposed Jameson deserved a chance to tell it. The two brothers walked the property for several hours. Their shoes kicked up small puffs of dust as they wandered through the groves. Jameson was quiet for the first fifteen minutes or so. Once he started talking the words came out in a steady stream. Walker listened intently without interjecting. When Jameson finally stopped speaking Walker was able to internally sum up the story in one phrase. *Living beyond one's means.* He didn't say this thought out loud however, he simply asked Jameson what he was going to do now.

"Can I stay with you for a while so I can get back on my feet?" Jameson asked.

"That's going to be up to Rita," Walker said.

"You're the man of the house, "Jameson began. When he saw Walker's face he stopped mid sentence. "You're right," he said instead, "it's up to her."

When they got back to the house Walker had Jameson wait on

the front porch while he went inside to talk to Rita. She listened to everything Walker had to say, then slowly shook her head.

"He's a bad influence Walker," she said, "I don't want him living in the same house as Loyal."

Walker nodded. He went to his desk and removed a check from the checkbook. He wrote Jameson a check for $1,000 and returned to his brother on the porch. Jameson accepted the check with a small nod, then turned and descended the stairs. Jameson drove away slowly, leaving a small dust trail rather than the usual cloud. Walker watched until the car disappeared from view.

47

LOYAL TRUESDALE

Loyal woke before Trinity. She looked so peaceful snuggled up in the warm covers. He thought briefly about staying in bed and getting a bit more sleep. In the end he decided to slide carefully out of the bed, leaving her to sleep while he made plans for the day ahead. His first order of business was getting dressed and lighting the fires. The snow had stopped falling during the night. The sun shone in the bright blue sky and reflected off the blanket of snow on the ground. The air was freezing. Once the fires were going Loyal brewed a pot of coffee and sat at the kitchen table to plan their day.

Francine had told him about the storage unit just as she was leaving last night. He supposed tackling that would be a good place to start. As he thought about that Loyal remembered the slippery and dangerous drive to the cabin the previous evening. Francine had told him his father had a snowplow. Loyal found a piece of paper and wrote a short note telling Trinity he was out looking for the snowplow. He pulled on his boots and, after a moment's hesitation, his father's heavy jacket. He found that the scent was not as upsetting to him as it had been the previous day.

The snowplow was easy to find. It was on the side of the shed and covered with a thick tarp. When he uncovered it Loyal was pleased to see that it looked fairly new. It was bright red and had the word BOSS on it. He folded the tarp and placed it inside the shed, just to the left of the door. Loyal spent a minute locating the model number then headed back inside where he found Trinity awake and sipping a cup of coffee in front of the fireplace.

"I found the plow," said Loyal. "I'm going to find a YouTube and learn how to hook it on to the truck."

"I'll make us some breakfast," said Trinity. "The weather app is indicating more snow by this afternoon. We've got six or seven hours of clear skies."

The plow had an automatic hydraulic lift system. Loyal attached it and plowed the drive. When he returned to the cabin he found a plate of crispy diced potatoes and steaming scrambled eggs waiting for him. Over breakfast Loyal told Trinity about Maynard Lily and the stolen investment money. He explained about Arnie Crenshaw, the distinctive ring, and the car accident. As an afterthought he told her about the bald man he had seen in the courtyard outside of Francine's office. By nine o'clock he and Trinity were in his truck and on the way to Francine Blackwater's office.

Loyal found parking in the same public lot he had used before.

He inserted four quarters and led Trinity to the lawyer's small office. They entered and found Francine sitting behind her desk and holding a phone to her ear. She smiled and waved them toward the chairs facing her desk.

"I know you don't like it Gregory," she said into the phone, "but I think it is your only option." She listened for a moment then said, "Okay, you think about it and get back to me." She disconnected the call and turned her attention to Loyal and Trinity.

"This is Trinity Glass," Loyal said. He turned to Trinity, "This is Francine Blackwater." The women shook hands across the desk then Francine looked at Loyal expectantly. "Thanks for getting me set up at the house," Loyal said. "It is very comfortable. I plowed the drive this morning."

"Excellent," said Francine. "What's the plan for today?"

"We'd like to tackle the storage unit while the weather is clear," said Loyal. "You mentioned having the key here."

Francine opened her desk drawer and produced a key. She handed it to Loyal. "The storage unit is just a few blocks from here," she said. It is called Hinds and Hinds." Francine reached in the drawer and came out with a business card. "Here's their information. The unit is number 56."

Loyal took the card and thanked Francine. When he and Trinity exited the office he pointed out the jewelry store across the courtyard explaining that that was the location where he had seen the bald man. Francine hadn't been joking when she had said the storage unit was close to her office. Less than ten minutes later Trinity and Loyal were parked in the parking lot and entering the office of Hinds and Hinds.

48

ANTONIO SHAW

The secluded location of the old man's house was both helpful and problematic. It had been helpful for the ambush. There had been no one to hear if the old man had cried out. He hadn't. It was problematic because there was no way to casually drive by and observe what was happening. Tony was pondering this as he sat at the end of Cavalry Drive waiting for the slow moving morning traffic to clear so that he could merge onto Paseo Del Pueblo Sur, the main road through the small town of Taos. He was trying to decide what action to take. He had searched the house and found no references to his grandfather. It was probably safe to leave Taos and head back to California, but something was telling him not to. Tony trusted his instincts, believing that they were the source of his tremendous luck.

Tony was unsurprised when luck struck once again. As he was watching the traffic pass him by, the rental truck the old man's son was driving passed directly in front of him. Tony was sure it was the same vehicle. He could see the son driving, but was surprised to see that a woman sat in the passenger seat. Tony accelerated into traffic two cars behind the truck and followed it until it parked in the same paid parking lot he had parked in when he had paid a visit to the attorney. Tony circled the block once and saw that the truck was still parked in the lot. He circled again and was pleased to see the truck waiting to pull out into traffic. It pulled out right behind him and followed him through the first stoplight. About a block after the stoplight the truck turned right into a parking lot. Tony took a quick left into the parking lot of a hardware store and watched as the truck parked in front of the office of a local storage unit.

Tony parked his vehicle so that he could watch them. The old man's son and the woman both slid out of the truck and went into the office. They were inside for less than ten minutes. When they exited the office they slid back into the truck and drove through the open gate and onto the property. Tony took a minute to digest what he had just witnessed. He came up with two options. The first was that the old man's son was going to empty his dad's house into a storage unit so that he could sell it. The second, and the one that gave Tony the chills, was that the old man had a storage unit and his son was about to open it.

Tony drove across the street and through the open gates of Hinds and Hinds. He drove methodically through the numerous rows of storage units. He was beginning to lose hope when he saw the rental truck parked outside of an open unit. He drove by slowly and registered the unit's number, 56, the fact that it was full of boxes, and that the old man's son and the woman were inside of it. Needing an excuse to come back to the unit Tony returned to the office and rented a unit for himself. He had noticed the many security cameras mounted on the units and wanted to avoid arousing suspicion. He managed to get a unit one row over from the old man's, paid cash for three months rent, and drove back to his Airbnb.

49

PATRICK O'KEEFE

Pat entered the sheriff's department through the back door. Olive hadn't been happy abut driving him back to his car. For a moment he had thought she was going to make him take an Uber, but she had relented and driven him to the Cow Shed parking lot. He went quickly up the stairs, entered his office, and closed the door. He wanted to lock the damn thing, but knew that would be regarded as suspicious if someone tried to enter. Instead he sat at his desk and opened his computer. He checked his emails then spent the better part of the morning working on other cases. Hammond's wasn't the only one he was involved with and he had been letting the other cases slide.

By one-thirty he had caught up on everything. Olive, who had packed him a lunch for years, had sent nothing with him today. He was hungover and hungry, but didn't want to leave the relative isolation of his office. He had made up his mind to hit up the Five Guys just South of Palomar Airport Road when

Hammond opened the door to his office and stepped in. He stopped abruptly when he saw Pat and said, "You look like shit."

"Head cold," said Pat.

Hammond narrowed his eyes and silently appraised Pat for a few seconds, then shrugged and said, "Uh huh." He stared at Pat for another few seconds then said, "I'm heading to San Diego to talk to Colleen's supervisor. You want to come?" Pat shook his head. "I'm waiting on the warrant for Frederick's medical records."

Hammond shrugged and walked out.

On the drive to Five Guys Pat called Olive. She let the call go to voicemail. Pat was disappointed, but not entirely surprised. He did not leave a message. Olive's mother had been a hopeless alcoholic. Her father had tried to take up the slack left by her mother's drunken absences, but he couldn't be everything his children needed. Her two younger brothers both struggled with substance abuse. Olive had a drink now and then, but a drunk for a husband was something she would never tolerate.

Five Guys did not have a drive through so Pat was forced to enter to get his food. He ordered it to go and ate it in his car. He hadn't realized how hungry he was and the food tasted delicious. The hangover was finally easing. On the drive back to the Sheriff's Department Pat called Olive again. Once more she let the call go to voicemail. This time Pat did leave a message telling her how sorry he was and how much he loved her. Just as he pulled into the parking lot his phone pinged. The message was from Olive telling him that she loved him too.

50

ANTONIO SHAW

Tony sat at the small dining room table in his rented condo and waited for the microwave to ding. He had picked up three orders of fajitas from El Conejo Cocina the previous day and was working his way through them. He had eaten the steak fajitas yesterday, was warming the chicken at the moment, and had a combo plate set aside for later. He was thinking about the storage unit and trying to decide whether or not to tell his grandfather about it. He had made the decision to call and check in when the microwave announced the food was ready.

Tony took half a dozen bites then dialed his grandfather's number. Audrey, the nurse, answered.

"Tony," she said, "are you back?"

"No Audrey," he said, "still in Taos. Is Grandpa awake?"

"Yes," she said, "but that trip to New Mexico took a lot out of him." She paused then added, "Only good news, ok Tony?"

"Ok."

It took a moment for his grandfather to get on the phone. Tony could hear Audrey murmuring to him and the rustling sound created as she helped him to sit up and made him comfortable.

"Tony," his grandfather said in a weak and whispery voice, "how is everything?"

"Good Grandpa," he said. "It looks like the old man's son is emptying the house. I saw him talking to a realtor, I think he's going to sell it."

His grandfather let out a long sigh. "That's good," he said, "that's the end of it then."

It was the first time in his life that Tony had lied to his grandfather. He felt his guts clench as the untrue words slipped out of his mouth. When he opened his mouth to speak again Audrey was on the phone.

"I think that's about all he can take right now," she said. There was a silence on the line, then she added, "Come home soon Tony."

Tony disconnected and set the phone on the table next to the fajitas. He pushed the plate away. His appetite had deserted him. He knew what Audrey was trying to tell him. His grandfather didn't have long to live.

51

TRINITY GLASS

Walker's storage unit was the largest Hinds and Hinds had to offer. It measured 10x20 and was located past the office and around the first set of units. The manager had laughed when he had told them that Walker had been one of their original customers. "He's had this unit since 1973," he had said. Loyal parked the truck in front of unit 56 and slid out. Trinity slid out as well and met him in front of the metal sliding door. She watched as Loyal slid the key into the lock and thought she detected a slight tremor in his hands. She supposed it could just be the chilly day. He glanced at her, she nodded, and he raised the door.

In much the same way that he kept his home neat and tidy, Walker had the storage unit arranged in an organized manner. To the right stood a wooden roll top desk. A chair sat in front of it and a file cabinet sat beside it. There was a small aisle between the desk and the rest of the unit, which was stacked chest high with boxes. Trinity and Loyal stood quietly for a moment, taking it all in. Trinity spoke first.

"How do you want to do this?" she asked.

Loyal sighed, then said, "I'll take the desk and file cabinet. Do you mind starting with the boxes?"

"That works," said Trinity. She watched Loyal walk over and sit in front of the desk then turned and pulled down the first box.

The first three boxes were full of records from the real estate sales Walker had made over the years. Trinity went through everything. She supposed Walker could have hidden a letter to Loyal among the papers and didn't want to miss anything. Going through all the papers required her to remove her gloves and after a little more than an hour her fingers were numb and clumsy. She placed the boxes she had gone through just outside the unit and walked back to check on Loyal. He was going through the desk methodically.

"How's it going?" Trinity asked. She was standing slightly behind him and to his right. He turned to look up at her.

"So far it has all been bank statements and financial records," he said. "Francine never mentioned bank accounts or stocks. I suppose she knew I would find everything here. Looks like he used this unit as his office."

Trinity nodded, "Everything I have seen so far has been sales records from his real estate business." She paused, then added, "My hands are freezing Loyal. I'm going to work on some boxes toward the back of the unit. It might be slightly warmer back there." Loyal nodded and turned back to the desk.

. . .

Walker had stacked the boxes with aisles between them, so everything was accessible without having to move things around. In the very back Trinity found a section of paintings. All were framed and wrapped in heavy blankets. Trinity looked through them quickly then rewrapped them. Loyal would have to look through these personally. If he didn't want them then it would require a bit of research to assess their value. She turned next to a cardboard box on the ground next to the paintings. She kneeled down, opened it, then rocked back on her heels as she let out a low breath. The cardboard box contained a wooden box. It looked to be handmade and a single word was burned into its lid...**RITA.**

Trinity wondered if she should get Loyal before she opened the box, but her curiosity got the better of her and she reached in and removed the wooden box. It was rough and had a bronze latch. There was no lock, so Trinity opened it. It was filled with small white boxes. With shaking hands Trinity reached in and picked one up. She opened it to find an exquisite ring inside. It was turquoise in a sliver band. The stone was an oval, a strip of twisted silver was wrapped delicately around it, and another single layer of silver wrapped around that. Three strips of silver branched out from each side of the turquoise and met together to form the band. Trinity opened some more of the boxes. All held beautiful pieces of jewelry; rings, bracelets, and necklaces. At the bottom of the box she found an unsigned birthday card.

Trinity replaced everything, lifted the box, and stood. She walked over to Loyal. He had finished with the desk and was working his way through the filing cabinet.

"Loyal," she said, "look at this."

He pushed away from the cabinet, stood, and turned toward her. She held the wooden box out and he took it from her. He sat back in the chair, held the box in his lap for a moment, then opened the lid. Trinity reached out, lifted a white box, and opened it.

"It's jewelry Loyal," she paused, "I think he bought a piece for your Mom's birthday each year." She held out the ring for him to see. It was the turquoise and silver one she had first opened. "It's so beautiful. Look at the detail."

Loyal pushed the wooden box back into Trinity's arms. He shook his head.

"Would have been nice if he had actually given them to her." He looked at Trinity. "Our birthdays were the hardest days of the year for her."

"At least now you know he was thinking about her." Trinity said. "Maybe that can help you get some closure and let some of the anger go."

From the way Loyal looked at her Trinity knew immediately she had said the wrong thing.

"I thought you came here to help, Trinity," he said roughly. "I don't need a God damn therapist right now."

Trinity tried to hide the hurt that surely showed on her face. She waited ten seconds to see if he was going to apologize, but Loyal remained silent.

"Right," she said as she turned away, "I'll just get back to work then."

The next half hour was spent in an uncomfortable silence.

Trinity found a box with some brochures about Taos from the 1970's and looked through them silently. The town had definitely grown in the last forty years. She was looking at a map of the historic district, produced by the Kiwanis Club of Taos in 1977, when Loyal's voice brought her back to the present. She turned and saw that he held Rita's wooden box in his hands.

"I'm going to take this to the jewelry store across from Francine's office to see what they think the value might be." He paused then added, "You want to come?"

Trinity shook her head. "No, I'll keep working."

"You sure," he said, "I might be gone a while."

Trinity looked at him. If this was an attempt at an apology it wasn't going to fly.

"Nope," she said, "I'll stay."

"You carrying?" Loyal asked.

"I'm a Federal agent Loyal," she said, "what do you think?"

52

LOYAL TRUESDALE

As Loyal drove he thought about his comment to Trinity. He knew it had stung and had seen the hurt in her eyes. He wasn't sure what had kept him from offering her an apology. By the time he parked in the paid parking and inserted eight quarters he had decided he would tell her he was sorry as soon as he got back to the storage unit. He grabbed the wooden box and headed for the jewelry store. When he opened the door of Tigua Treasures a small chime announced his presence. A young woman looked up from behind the counter and smiled at him

"Welcome to Tigua Treasures," she said.

Loyal smiled back as he walked to the counter.

"I'm going through my dad's things," he said. "I have some jewelry I was hoping you could look at. Maybe give me an idea of the value?"

He set the box on the counter and opened the lid. "There's thirty-seven pieces."

"I'll take a quick peek," the woman said. "This type of thing isn't really what I do."

. . .

By the time she had opened a dozen boxes the woman's attitude had changed. "You've got some really nice pieces here Mr.." As her voice trailed off Loyal realized he had never given her his name.

"Loyal," he said, "Loyal Truesdale."

"I'm Onawa Shanley," she said. "Do you have some time?" she asked. "I'd like to look through everything."

Loyal nodded. Onawa walked to the door and turned the sign from *open* to *closed*. She indicated a visitor's chair. Loyal removed his coat and sat. He thought about calling Trinity and apologizing over the phone, but decided to wait and talk to her in person.

Loyal watched as Onawa examined each piece. She often used her jeweler's loupe to look at small details. As she moved the boxes around Loyal could see that she was sorting the pieces into different groups. More than an hour passed before she turned her gaze on Loyal again.

"This is a valuable collection Mr. Truesdale," she said. "I took over this store from my grandma over five years ago." She indicated one group, "These pieces are hers and they are signed. She is a famous artist and no longer produces pieces. These are worth a lot." She indicated another group of boxes. "These pieces are from local artists, some are alive and some have passed. All these are signed as well." She pointed to the last group. "These are not signed, but are of excellent quality."

. . .

Loyal thought about this for a minute or so then said, "Make me an offer Ms. Shanley. I'd like to sell them."

"You could make much more money if you sold them yourself," she said.

Loyal sighed, "I wouldn't know where to begin. I'm only in Taos for a few days."

"Any offer I give you will be ridiculously low," Onawa said.

"What does ridiculously low sound like?" said Loyal.

Onawa looked at all the boxes in front of her, then back up at Loyal. "I can't go any higher than $22,750."

Loyal didn't even try to hide his shock. He thought about Trinity, and the look on her face as she had held the turquoise ring. He stood, found the ring in the group of pieces made by Onawa's grandmother, and picked it up.

"I'd like to keep this one," he said, "and maybe you could help me pick out something else for my daughter."

As Loyal was walking to his truck, two white boxes and a check for $20,300 in the wooden box, a thought occurred to him. He placed the wooden box in his truck and retrieved the pictures of Damien Sallwell and his ring. He returned to Tigua Treasures. Onawa looked up in surprise when he walked in.

"I was wondering if you could look at one more thing for me," he said as he held out the two pieces of paper. She took them from him. He noticed her eyes widen slightly.

"I'm not sure I understand Mr. Truesdale."

"Have you ever seen that man or that ring?" he asked.

Onawa looked down again. She took her jeweler's loupe and studied both pictures. She shook her head when she looked up again. "Sorry, no."

Loyal accepted the pictures back from her, thanked her again for everything, and exited the shop. He turned back when he had gone about five paces and looked through the window. He could see Onawa Shanley. She had her back to the window and a phone in her hand.

53

DEAN HAMILTON

Hamilton had just come in from plowing his drive when his phone rang. He looked at caller ID, saw it was Onawa, and answered.

"Onawa," he said, "you design something for me already?"

"Dean," she said, "I just had a strange experience. A man showed me two pictures. One was definitely your ring, the one Marci made you." She paused then continued. "The other was a picture of a man whose body could be yours, but the face doesn't match."

"I was mugged in Arizona last week Onawa," Hamilton said. "They got the ring. The guy had a mask on, but he was about my size. It was his gun that convinced me to cooperate."

"I'm so sorry Dean," said Onawa, "I didn't know that. I told him I didn't recognize the man in the picture or the ring."

"Did the man leave his contact information?" asked Hamilton.

"I have his name and number," said Onawa. "He told me he is emptying out his father's estate. The collection of jewelry he brought in is quite valuable. He even has some of grandma's pieces. He kept two and I bought the rest."

"Maybe he has information about my ring," Hamilton said.

Onawa rattled off Loyal's name and phone number and they disconnected.

Hamilton stood in silent thought for several minutes. He had been lucky with Arnie Crenshaw and the car accident. Staging another would be risky. He decided his best move would be to research this Loyal Truesdale and learn more about the man before picking a strategy with which to eliminate him. Hamilton shrugged off the coat he was still wearing and hung it on the rack. He removed his boots and left them on the floor in the entry way. Not knowing how long his research would take him, he prepared a roast beef sandwich and took it and a beer into his study. He lit a fire in the potbelly stove near his desk and settled in at his computer.

Two hours later Hamilton had quite a resume on Loyal Truesdale and deep concerns. The man was a retired homicide detective. His career with the Carlsbad Sheriff's Department was noteworthy. Hamilton had accessed the department's personnel files and was not happy to read about Truesdale's higher than average solve rate or his glowing reviews by superior officers. Another thing that caught Hamilton's attention was Truesdale's recent purchase of a home that was valued at just over one million dollars. Unless the man had received an extremely large inheritance, the detective's pension could not support that kind of purchase. He called Onawa back.

"Hey," he said as casually as he could manage, "have you showed your grandma those pieces that you bought today?"

"Not yet," said Onawa, "I'm going over there after I close the shop. Why?"

"Just curious," said Hamilton, "be interesting to know who accumulated such a comprehensive collection."

"Yeah," said Onawa, "I'm curious too. I'll call you if I find out."

Hamilton finished the sandwich and the beer and cleared away the debris. He brought another beer back into the study, fed some logs into the potbelly stove, and settled back in front of his computer. A study of Truesdale's personal life revealed two divorces and one daughter. He took a quick peek at the daughter and learned of the recent birth of little Mason. Hamilton leaned back in his chair and thought about everything he had learned. He realized that Truesdale, coming from California, had likely flown and rented a vehicle. This search was simple and soon he had Loyal's one way flight information as well as the make, model, and license plate of his rental truck. An added bonus was that GMC, the maker of his truck, owned Onstar. With another quick hack Hamilton located Truesdale's rental truck in real time.

54

LOYAL TRUESDALE

As Loyal drove back to the storage unit he replayed a conversation with Maynard Lily in his mind. He was quite sure Maynard had said that Arnie Crenshaw had told him he was leaving Santa Fe and going to Taos to meet with someone who may have had information about the ring on Damien Sallwell's hand. He pictured Onawa in his mind, back to him and phone in her hand. Her eyes had widened when she had seen the pictures of Sallwell and the ring. Loyal was fairly sure she was lying about recognizing either one.

He braked hard in front of unit 56, slid out and went to find Trinity. He found her where he had left her, in the back of the unit going through boxes. The one she had open in front of her was filled with clay figurines.

"We need to get back to the house," Loyal said. She looked at him with undisguised annoyance and said, "We still have a few hours before the snow starts up again."

"We need to go now Trinity," he said. He glanced around.

"Let's pack up the art and the box you are working on. We can finish at home."

"Loyal...," Trinity began but he cut her off. "Please, I'm sorry about before." He paused then added, "Really, I am. I'd just feel better if we were back at the house."

Trinity gave him a strange look and, with a small sigh, stood. "Ok," she said, "let's pack it all up.

In less than twenty minutes they had the art and figurines in the truck and the unit locked back up. Loyal drove out of town with an urgency he couldn't quite explain. He was grateful that Trinity didn't ask. Snow was just beginning to fall when they reached Walker's home. They worked quickly and silently to bring everything into the house. Loyal got both fires going then asked Trinity to sit at the kitchen table with him. He told her first about Onawa and the jewelry sale.

"You sold everything?" she asked. Loyal nodded. "Except these," he said. He opened the wooden box and handed Trinity a white box. She opened it and saw the ring.

"It's for you," he said. "I'm sorry for what I said earlier Trinity. You dropped everything to come out here and help me." He looked at her for a long moment then said, "Forgive me?"

She met his gaze then slowly nodded. "What else is going on Loyal," she said, "you got us out of Hinds and Hinds in record time."

Loyal's phone rang just as he opened his mouth to explain his reasoning to her. He glanced at the screen, saw it was Dwight Crenshaw, and accepted.

"Hello," he said.

"Mr. Truesdale," Dwight said, "it is Dwight Crenshaw. I just wanted to call and let you know that my dad passed away this afternoon."

"I'm sorry," said Loyal and he meant it.

"I made a choice not to have my dad in my life," said Dwight, his voice tight with emotion, "and I don't regret that. I'm still glad he heard a friendly voice before he died."

Dwight cut the connection before Loyal had a chance to respond. He looked at Trinity and said, "The PI I told you about, Arnie Crenshaw? He died today." Loyal reached out and took her hands in his. "I'm starting to think his accident wasn't as accidental as everyone thinks," he said. He proceeded to tell Trinity about Onawa Shanley's reaction to the pictures of Sallwell and his ring. "She was on the phone less than a minute after I left," he said. "She has my name and phone number from the jewelry sale. I thought it best for us to get back here as quickly as possible."

Trinity agreed with Loyal's assessment of the situation. "You know I don't believe in coincidences Loyal," she said. "I mean the odds of Sallwell being in Taos at the same time as you are astronomical." She paused, "And yet, here we are. I trust your instincts. If Sallwell is here and knows that you are asking about him then we need to make sure we are secure." Trinity and Loyal spent the next half hour searching the house and shed. In the very back of the bedroom closet Loyal found an 18 inch barreled Mossberg 590 pump shotgun. Ammunition, a vertical grip, and an attachable flashlight were stored beside it. Loyal couldn't help but smile when he found it. He realized that this was the first smile related to his father that he had experienced since he was eleven years old.

55

DEAN HAMILTON

Hamilton was working his way through a filet mignon when his phone rang. The caller ID indicated Onawa Shanley and he accepted.

"Onawa," he said.

"Hi Dean," Onawa said, "I'm at my grandma's. She kept very thorough records. The person who she designed the rings for is named Dale Walker."

"That's interesting stuff, Onawa," Hamilton said. "Say hi to your grandma for me ok?"

Hamilton disconnected before Onawa had a chance to respond. He knew it had been rude of him and made a mental note to make a large purchase from her shop soon.

Hamilton learned quickly that Dale Walker had passed away just over a week ago. As he researched the man's past a few more nuggets of information were revealed. He owned a home just outside of Taos. Interestingly the address was the same as the address where, according to Onstar, Loyal Truesdale currently was. Dale Walker had sold real estate in the Taos area for many years. Hamilton accessed some documents that had Walker's office address on them. A quick Google search informed him that Walker had shared office space with Francine Blackwater, Attorney at Law, in historic downtown Taos. Hamilton found no images of Dale Walker, the only exception being his New Mexico driver's license which had been originally applied for in July of 1972. Prior to this date Hamilton could find no information about Dale Walker. It took another half hour but eventually Hamilton found that Dale Walker's social security number had originally been issued in 1932 to a boy from Indiana named named Oscar Olsen. Oscar had died in 1934.

Hamilton pondered this information for a moment then returned to Loyal Truesdale. He accessed Loyal's birth certificate. Loyal's parents were listed as Rita Truesdale, maiden name Mason, and Walker Truesdale. A smile spread slowly across Hamilton's face. He wrote the names *Dale Walker/Walker Truesdale* on a note pad on his desk, then began his research into Walker Truesdale. Once he had Walker's social security number the rest was easy for Hamilton. He learned that Walker had been an engineer with Boeing in Seattle in the 1950's. He found some articles from the local newspaper highlighting the 727 project. Walker's name was listed as one of the top engineers. Walker left Boeing and relocated to Fallbrook, California in 1959. Hamilton found the marriage certificate for Walker and Rita and learned that Walker had begun working for General Dynamics.

. . .

Walker had resigned from General Dynamics in March of 1972 and basically disappeared. In spite of his tremendous skills with computers, Hamilton could find nothing until the man reappeared as Dale Walker in Taos in July of 1972. Four months of utter silence and then the metamorphosis from Walker Truesdale to Dale Walker had occurred. Hamilton leaned back in his chair and closed his eyes. His mind worked in much the same way as a computer. He sat and let it do its work, organizing and compartmentalizing all the information he had just ingested. After a full five minutes of silence he opened his eyes and stood. His next step had been decided. He walked out of the study and began to prepare.

56

TRINITY GLASS

Trinity stirred the Bertolli frozen shrimp scampi and linguini on the stovetop. Her eyes were on the food but her mind was elsewhere. The white box containing the turquoise ring sat on the kitchen table. Loyal was in the living room chair examining the shotgun he had found in his father's closet. She couldn't see him from where she stood but from the sounds she was hearing she could tell he was loading it. She wasn't convinced about his theory that they might be in danger, but Loyal was not prone to flights of fancy, so she was taking him seriously.

Her mind slipped back to the moment in the storage unit when he had snapped at her. They had been together nearly nine months now. Admittedly, their actual time spent with each other was quite a bit less than that, but they talked or texted most days if they could. This was the first time she had seen this side of him. The situation with his father was beyond difficult and she was trying to be understanding of that. Still, she had angered her boss by leaving Texas for three days to come to New Mexico to support him and didn't appreciate his snarky comment about not needing a therapist.

The sizzling from the pan brought Trinity out of her reverie and back to her task at hand; not burning dinner. She removed the pan from the heat and placed the lid on it. She set two bowls on the counter. She filled two glasses with water and set them on the kitchen table then rounded the corner to let Loyal know dinner was ready. He was sitting in the large chair that fronted the fireplace. He had turned it so that it faced the front door rather than the flames. He sat still, staring off into space. The shotgun lay across his lap.

"Dinner's ready," she said.

He looked up at her, stood, and set the shotgun back on the chair.

"You think I'm over thinking everything?" he asked.

"Honestly Loyal," she said, "I don't know what to think. If Onawa Shanley did recognize the ring and called its owner then we could be in danger. Arnie Crenshaw was on his way to Taos to talk to someone about the ring and he lost his life."

Loyal closed the space between them and wrapped his arms around her.

"I'd rather be wrong and safe," he said.

As they ate dinner they made plans for the next day. Thursday was Trinity's last full day in New Mexico. Her flight was scheduled for 9:15 on Friday morning. She was planning on leaving Taos at 5:30 am to allow time to return the rental vehicle and to check her bag with the firearm inside.

"Loyal," Trinity said, "can I see the picture of Sallwell's ring again?"

Loyal pulled it out of his pocket, unfolded it, and lay it on the table oriented toward her. She looked at it for a moment then raised her head and looked at Loyal.

"I have a colleague I'd like to email this picture to," she said. "Maybe it has shown up in previous investigations. Sallwell stole thirty million dollars. He likely started with smaller amounts. This can't be his first crime."

Trinity connected her phone to her laptop and created a hot spot. She took a picture of Sallwell's ring and sent it off in an email. She and Loyal spent then next several hours sorting and cataloging the paintings and figurines from the storage unit. All were dated and signed. The hot spot worked well and Trinity was able to research the artists. By 11:30 they had created a comprehensive list. Loyal had picked out a few pieces that he wanted to keep for himself. Trinity had chosen a watercolor depicting a sunset. The artist was Hyde Solomon. He was well known for his watercolors depicting sunrises and sunsets in Taos. This particular piece was 56"x64". It had been painted in 1974 and was signed. When Trinity saw the approximate value she tried to give it back to Loyal.

"I want you to have it Trinity," he said.

57

PATRICK O'KEEFE

Pat woke just before 2:00 am. The house was dark and quiet. He could hear Ava making small snuffling sounds as she slept in her bassinet. Olive was rolled onto her left side and was facing away from him. Her gentle breaths were light and even. He could tell that she was asleep. After the kids had gone to sleep they had sat in front of the fireplace and talked. Pat had explained his feelings of disillusionment, how he wanted to believe the best about people but was struggling. Olive had listened in her usual way, focusing on his words and really hearing him. They had talked about her mother and her brothers and their struggle with substance abuse. By the time they went to bed they had worked things out.

Pat slid out of bed and went to the kitchen. On the way he peeked into both Sullivan's and Piper's rooms. They were deep asleep, their faces relaxed and their breathing calm and even. Pat sat at the kitchen table and thought about Colleen and

Frederick Young. He was hoping that the warrant for Frederick's medical records would come through today. He had asked for access to the data from the pacemaker from four hours before the fire broke out. If Frederick was lying and he had not been asleep during that window of time the pacemaker data would reveal his deception. Pat was hoping that he would find that Frederick was telling the truth, but had to admit to himself that he believed the man was lying. Hammond had stopped by his office after meeting with Colleen and Frederick's supervisor. The woman had said that both were hard workers and excellent employees. When pressed, she had admitted that Colleen's performance had suffered during the past year. She had told Hammond that she hadn't wanted to speak ill of the dead. Realizing that sleep was lost to him, Pat brewed some coffee, opened his lap top, and began to work.

58

LOYAL TRUESDALE

Loyal and Trinity had agreed that someone should stay awake during the night to keep watch. Loyal had taken first watch. He was sitting in the living room in his father's large chair. He had let the fire die down, but heat still radiated from the stones surrounding the fireplace. He had the chair turned toward the front door. The blinds were covering all the windows with the exception of a narrow rectangular window next to the front door. Trinity was asleep in the bedroom. They had left the fire in that room burning.

They had agreed that Loyal would wake Trinity at 2:00 am and she would take the second shift. Loyal did not plan on leaving her alone to guard the house, but just after 2:00 he slipped into the bedroom to check on her. He carried the shotgun with him. He could see Trinity by the light of the dying fire. She lay on her left side. Her hair was loose and flowed across the blankets. When lit by the dwindling flames it looked like a river of lava. Loyal couldn't help but smile when he remembered the nickname he had given her before he actually met her; Ginger/Cinnamon. He moved closer. He was thinking about waking her when he saw her right hand. It was tucked underneath the pillow. Only two fingers were exposed, her pinkie and her ring finger. In the dim light he could see the turquoise ring on her finger. With a small smile Loyal slipped out of the bedroom. He went to the kitchen and started another pot of coffee. If the aroma didn't wake her then he would let her sleep.

59

DEAN HAMILTON

Hamilton believed in preparation. The more one knew about his quarry the better. His online research regarding Loyal Truesdale was helpful, but he wanted to see the man in his element. He dressed in layers starting with long underwear then slipping into Iron-Tuff coveralls. He slid his feet into a pair of Scarpa Phantom 8000 Mountaineering Boots. They had cost over $800 and he had found them to be well worth the price. He packed a handful of disposable hand warmers, a 300 yard reel of double braid polyester rope, a helmet, and a pair of starlight night vision goggles with a helmet mount into his truck. He engaged the plow attachment but kept it raised. His 1911 series Kimber .45ACP, the Stainless Steel Raptor, was safely stowed in the right front zippered pocket of his coveralls. The snow was still falling, but less heavily, when Hamilton left his house and headed toward Walker Truesdale's home.

Hamilton parked the truck in the cover of some trees at the

edge of Truesdale's property. He tied one end of the rope to a belt loop on the coveralls. He left the spool on the driver's seat and the truck window lowered just enough for the rope to slip through the small space. He was leaving nothing to chance. Heavy snow was predicted in the next few hours and he wanted to make sure he could find his way back to his vehicle. He slipped the helmet onto his head. It covered the top of his head and sat above his ears. The starlight goggles were attached to the helmet and had a hinge that allowed them to be raised and lowered. He double checked that his Kimber was stowed properly in his pocket, lowered the goggles, and began the walk to Truesdale's home.

Hamilton had reviewed the property details closely. The road to the house was just over 200 yards long. He had studied the plans and memorized the details of the house's layout. He assumed Loyal would be asleep in the bedroom. His plan was to approach from the opposite side of the house and work his way around. He hadn't decided yet how he wanted to eliminate Loyal Truesdale. Using his Kimber would be easy and effective, but would open up an investigation and he would have to get rid of the gun. He had purchased it using an alias and doubted it could be traced back to him. Still, one of the reasons he had never been caught was his attention to detail.

The snowfall was picking up as he made his way toward the house. It made no difference to Hamilton. His starlight goggles illuminated everything around him. He approached the shed and made his way around the back of it. He stopped at the edge and focused his vision on the house. He knew there were only two entrances, the front door and a door that led into the mudroom just off the kitchen. The house was dark. The front room window's blinds were lowered. There was, however, a narrow rectangular window next to the front door that had no cover. Hamilton activated the zoom feature on the goggles. He was surprised to see Truesdale, awake, and sitting ramrod straight in a large chair facing the front door. A shotgun lay in his lap. As Hamilton watched, Truesdale stood and walked out of the narrow view provided by the window. Hamilton knew the layout of the house. Truesdale was heading to the bathroom or the bedroom.

He reappeared less than two minutes later, crossed Hamilton's field of view, and disappeared into what Hamilton knew to be the kitchen. While he waited for Truesdale to reappear, Hamilton considered what he was seeing. The man was clearly expecting something. Although Onawa had assured him that she had said nothing, a seasoned detective like Truesdale would have noticed even the smallest of signs. Maybe her eyes had widened when she had seen the picture. Perhaps she had taken in the slightest breath or her hands had trembled as she examined the picture and handed it back. The how didn't matter, then end result was the same. Truesdale was prepared.

When Truesdale re-entered Hamilton's vision he was carrying the shotgun in his left hand and and a steaming mug in his right. He sat back in the chair, placed the shotgun in his lap, and sipped what Hamilton assumed to be coffee. Hamilton watched and thought. The falling snow did not obstruct his view and he was sure Truesdale could not see him. Every inch of his body, with the exception of his jawline and mouth was covered. The exposed skin was cold and he was considering activating the disposable hand warmers he had in his chest pocket when the woman appeared beside Truesdale. Her gray pajamas hung loosely on her slender frame. A river of tousled copper hair flowed down her back. Her skin was pale. She leaned down as Truesdale looked up and gently kissed him on the lips. Hamilton felt a surge of unexpected rage flow through his body. Truesdale held up the mug. She nodded, accepted it from him, and raised it to her lips. Hamilton watched as she sipped and swallowed. The optics on the goggles were of such fine quality that he could see the movement in the hollow of her neck as she swallowed. Unaware that he was doing so, Hamilton began moving forward. The woman was exquisite. His eyes were just working their way down to the shape of her breasts when he was blinded by a sudden light.

Instinctively Hamilton closed his eyes and dropped flat on the ground. He worked his way backwards in a reverse army crawl motion until his foot bumped into the edge of the shed. Despite the fact that his eyes were still closed, bright red and purple flashes assaulted his vision. He worked his way behind the shed, then sat up and raised the goggles. He opened his eyes. His vision was definitely impaired. He reached down and grasped the rope where it was attached to the belt loop then stood, and using it as a guide, he began working his way back to his truck.

60

TRINITY GLASS

Trinity was just handing the mug back to Loyal when the motion sensor lights came on in the front of the house. In a swift movement Loyal was out of the chair and had moved them toward the bathroom.

"An animal?" Trinity whispered.

"Possibly," said Loyal.

"If you want to go look at least let me cover you," she said.

Trinity turned and slipped into the bedroom. She grabbed her Sig Sauer Compact 45 off the end table and returned to Loyal.

"I just need my jacket and boots," she said. "They are by the front door. I can find them without lights."

"The outside lights turned back off," said Loyal. "If it is a person they could be behind the shed. The motion sensors aren't tripped if we stand on the porch. The activation point is about five feet out."

Trinity nodded, then realizing Loyal couldn't see her well in the dark, added "Ok, how do you want to do this?"

"I want to go out the mudroom and around the side of the

house," said Loyal "We can pick a spot and trip the lights again. If it is a person it should take them by surprise."

Trinity worked her way over to the the front door and slipped her boots and jacket on. She retrieved a black beanie from the jacket pocket, slipped it on her head, and tucked her hair underneath it. She returned to Loyal and together they made their way through the kitchen and to the mudroom door. Loyal opened it cautiously and they stepped out into the night. There was a slight breeze and the falling snow swirled around Trinity as she followed Loyal towards the front of the house. He was dressed in black and nearly invisible. She sensed his movement more than she actually saw it. Trinity thought about how she would have approached this house on a night like this. Starlight night vision goggles came to mind immediately. If someone had been out there and tripped the lights while wearing night vision they would definitely be having vision issues.

Loyal planned their placement perfectly and when the lights activated the house was behind them and the shed and driveway were illuminated. The lights were bright and Trinity could see the shed fairly well despite the snow coming from the sky. She watched as Loyal knelt down and examined something in the snow. Trinity eased forward and looked down. Something had clearly been laying in the snow. There was a depression that was quickly filling. It looked as if something had been dragged through the snow toward the shed. Rising and stepping to the side, Loyal walked beside the depression to the back edge of the shed. He turned on the flashlight that was attached to the shotgun. Trinity followed two feet behind him. The edge of the shed was more protected from the snowfall. Trinity could see clearly that something had been sitting on the ground here. Loyal leaned down and picked something up. He turned to her and opened his hand. In it he held a disposable hand warmer.

Trinity and Loyal followed bootprints that led from the shed to the main road two hundred yards away from the house. They thought they could make out some tire tracks, but couldn't definitively attribute them to whomever had been observing the house. They spent a few minutes looking both directions down the road, then walked back up the drive to the house. They re-entered through the mud room, which they had left unlocked. They quickly cleared the house and found it to be empty. Loyal started fires in both fireplaces while Trinity held her numb hands under a stream of hot water in the kitchen sink. When she felt a tingling sensation in her hands Trinity turned off the water. She poured herself a cup of coffee and joined Loyal in the living room. He was standing in front of the the fireplace. He held the disposable hand warmer in his hand.

"I shouldn't have picked it up," he said. "There might be prints."

"Doubtful," said Trinity. "Whoever was out there had to have been wearing gloves. My hands became completely numb during the short time we were out there."

"Still," said Loyal, "a mistake on my part."

Trinity crossed the room and stood beside him with her back to the fire.

"The ring is the common thread," she said.

Loyal nodded. "Agreed," he said. "The art community here is tight knit. I don't think anyone is going to tell us anything about the owner."

"It had to have been him or her out there tonight," Trinity said. "Animals don't carry hand warmers."

Loyal gave a small laugh. "Nope," he said.

"If it was me doing surveillance on this house I would have used Starlight night vision," Trinity said. "If our unsub was, they are having vision issues at the moment." She paused, then added, "I think we should carry on with our plans. Act like we don't suspect anything but be prepared for everything."

Loyal slid his arm around her and pulled her in tight. "I agree. And if Arnie's accident was not an accident then our guy is pretty sophisticated." He turned so that they were facing each other. "It is just after 3:00 am," he said. "Sun comes up around 6:30. I don't think our guy is going to be back tonight. Want to go back to bed?"

Trinity leaned up and kissed his chin. "That's the best idea you have had today," she said. She took his hand and led him to the bedroom.

61

DEAN HAMILTON

The drive back to the house was dangerous. Red and purple light flashed continuously in Hamilton's vision. When he pulled into his garage he was equal parts relieved and furious. His anger was multifaceted. First, he was angry with himself for not suspecting motion activated lighting. Such lighting was unusual in mountain dwellings where nocturnal animals of all types and sizes roamed freely. The way the sensors were positioned so far from the house was unusual as well. The second aspect of his anger was directed at Loyal Truesdale. Specifically at the kiss he had shared with the woman. Hamilton understood that his reaction was bizarre. He did not know the woman. They had no connection and he could not lay any claim on her. His reaction to the kiss had been a gut level response, illogical and unfounded. Still, it existed.

Hamilton let himself into his home and went straight to the bathroom. He turned on the water to his claw footed bath tub and let it heat while he undressed. He removed the Kimber from the front pocket of the coveralls and set it on the sink. He reached into his upper pocket to remove the two hand warmers he had placed in it and came up with only one. He closed his eyes and went through the evening in his mind. The pocket wasn't zippered. One must have fallen out while he was belly crawling backwards toward the shed. Truesdale would find it if that was the case. Hamilton had handled it with gloves on so no fingerprints would be on it. It was a problem though, because Truesdale would know it had been a human that triggered the lights, not an animal.

Hamilton dimmed the bathroom lights and slipped into the hot water. The tub was large and he was able to submerge his entire body. The only thing exposed was his face. He sat this way for a long time, eyes closed and breathing slowly. He let his thoughts drift. Images of Walker Truesdale/Dale Walker kept floating by. The man had left his old life and created a brand new identity for a reason. The way he had installed his sensor lights intrigued Hamilton. Normally lights such as those would be close to the house, but Walker had installed them some distance from the house. Almost like a first line of defense against an attack. By the time he had pulled the plug on the tub and was toweling himself off Hamilton had decided more research on Walker was necessary. He had also decided to find out the identity of the woman in Loyal Truesdale's house.

62

PATRICK O'KEEFE

Olive entered the kitchen just after 6:00. She carried Ava in her arms. Pat looked up at her and smiled.

"Couldn't sleep?" she asked.

"Nope," he said, "I was trying not to wake you."

"You didn't," said Olive. She held Ava out toward him. "She did."

Pat took Ava from Olive and held his daughter close to his chest. The fuzz of her hair was red like his own. She looked up at him and met his gaze with her incredibly blue eyes. Pat looked back at her for a minute or so, then kissed her forehead and raised his eyes to look at Olive. She had her back toward him and was measuring coffee grounds into the coffee maker to start a fresh pot. Once she had pushed the start button she turned around and faced him.

"What time did you get up?" she asked.

Pat shrugged. "2:00 ish?"

"You get any work done?" Olive asked.

"Some," said Pat as he stood and handed Ava back to her mother. He kissed Olive gently on the cheek.

"Time for me to get a shower," he said. "I'm hoping for the pacemaker warrant today."

By 7:15 Pat was showered, dressed, and in his car heading to Carlsbad. A lunch prepared by Olive sat on the passenger seat. Every time he looked at it he smiled. He parked in the back and entered through the back door. His first stop was Hammond's office. It was empty. Pat walked back down the hall and entered his own office. He opened his computer and looked again at the two pictures of Colleen Young; the first so happy the second so sad. He thought about Olive, his beautiful and generous wife. She was the best person he had ever known. He wondered what had happened in Colleen and Frederick's life for such a transition to have taken place and made a silent promise never to allow that to happen in his own marriage.

63

WALKER TRUESDALE - AUGUST 1971

Walker had heard little from his brother since he had given him the check and sent him on his way. Jameson had called on Christmas to say hello. Their conversation had been brief. He had called again on Loyal's birthday to wish his nephew a happy day. To say Walker was surprised, and happy, to hear from Jameson in August was an understatement. His younger brother, sounding upbeat and happy, had invited Walker to attend the Del Mar horse races with him and a friend. The friend had a box, he had said. They would be betting in style and comfort. Rita had not been thrilled to hear that Jameson was gambling. It was one of the few fights they had had in their life together. In the end Walker flat out told her he was going whether she liked it or not. Rita had not liked it.

Jameson picked Walker up in a brand new bright red Porsche 911T. Walker saw Rita roll her eyes when Jameson drove down the driveway in a cloud of dust. "He's up to his old tricks Walker," she said. "This can't end well."

"I'm just going to spend the day with him," Walker said. "I promise I won't give him any money or invite him to stay with us." He kissed her on the lips and walked to the front door. As he opened it he turned and said, "If he's drunk by the end of the day I'll get a taxi home, okay?"

Walker squeezed his tall frame into the tiny car and turned to look at his brother. Jameson was dressed in a red corduroy suit with a white shirt beneath the jacket. His hair was longer than Walker had ever seen it. He wore a large square pair of sunglasses with the words *Ray Ban* in the upper corner of the right lens. He was wearing an aftershave that threatened to make Walker's eyes water.

"Hey bro," said Jameson. He looked Walker up and down. "Don't you ever get new clothes?"

Walker looked down at the suit he was wearing. He tried to remember when he had purchased it and figured it was at least seven years old. He looked back at his brother and shook his head. Jameson laughed. He shifted into first, spun a u-turn, and roared back down the driveway.

The friend who owned the box at Del Mar was named Marco Barrossa. Jameson introduced him as a friend and business partner. When Barrossa shook Walker's hand his hand was warm and dry, his grip firm. They were seated at a table in the exclusive Turf Club on the fourth level, high above the masses of plebeian betters below. Walker ordered whiskey straight up and water on the side. A wide variety of sea food appetizers were spread across the table. Barrossa had a man who placed their bets for them. Walker sipped the whiskey and the water and placed conservative bets. He didn't know what type of bets Barrossa was making, but did notice that the man drank only coffee. Jameson drank multiple Jack and coke's and placed extravagant bets. Some were winners and some were losers. Walker didn't know how Jameson had fared overall at the end of the day. What he had noticed was Barrossa's keen eyes following all of Jameson's actions.

At the end of the day Walker thanked Barrossa for allowing him to be included in the day's racing. Jameson insisted a picture of the three men be taken with the camera he had brought along. The man who had placed their bets for them took the picture. Barrossa stood in the middle with Walker on one side and Jameson on the other.

64

DEAN HAMILTON

Dean Hamilton was not Hamilton's original name, nor was Arnie Crenshaw Hamilton's original murder victim. Hamilton had been born in 1978 and given the name Gordon Walsh by his parents. He had grown up in Ann Arbor, Michigan. His childhood had been typically middle class. Both parents were teachers and he had two sisters seven and eight years his junior. Gordon graduated at the top of his class and was accepted at MIT. He left his family behind without a backwards glance. Although Gordon's major was computer science, he found himself immediately drawn into the darker side of the Internet and his ability to manipulate things. By the end of his second year he was rarely actually attending classes. He used his skills to manipulate his grades. He returned to his family home every Thanksgiving and Christmas but spent his summer's in Massachusetts.

During the summer between his second and third year Gordon did two things. First, he manipulated the roommate selection so that he ended up with Charlie Hauser, a sophomore and, more importantly to Gordon, an orphan. Second, he began to work out. By the time he and Charlie actually met, Gordon was no longer skinny. When Thanksgiving rolled around Gordon returned to Ann Arbor. While there he purchased an older car and parked it in an isolated spot about three miles from his parent's house. His parent's lived on the edge of a large wooded area. He could walk from their house to the car without being seen.

At Christmas Gordon invited Charlie to come home with him. During the days leading up to Christmas Eve Gordon found himself repulsed by his family and the small, boring life he felt they led. Charlie was loving every minute he spent with the Walsh family. They went on hikes during the day, cooked together, and played board games in the evening. Gordon spent his time with his computer. On Christmas Eve Gordon poured the glasses of eggnog for the traditional toast. Using his computer skills he had gotten a prescription for a tranquilizer used in veterinary offices. He poured a healthy dose in each eggnog, with the exception of his. Twenty minutes after the family toast Gordon's father, mother, two sisters, and Charlie were all asleep in their chairs.

It took Gordon longer than he had anticipated to maneuver his sleeping family and guest into their respective rooms. Despite the strength training he had been doing, he struggled getting the limp forms into the beds. He opened his father's gun safe and was surprised and pleased to find nearly $6,000.00 in cash as well as the guns and ammo. He stuffed everything into a large duffel bag. Once he had everything he wanted he splashed gasoline in every room. He didn't care if the police knew it was arson. He hoped they would assume that Charlie was Gordon, beyond that he did not care. It was time for him to move on. The house went up like a match. Gordon walked the three miles to his car, eased it down the access road until it hit the highway, and drove away. Without a second thought he left Gordon Walsh behind and began his new life as Timothy Freeman.

65

DEAN HAMILTON

Timothy Freeman settled in Nashville, Tennessee. He got a job as a bartender and rented a one bedroom apartment. When he wasn't working in the bar he was working on his computer. He became quite adept at stealing credit card information. Sometimes he stole entire identities. He learned how to get in bank's electronic back doors and quietly withdrew random amounts from various accounts. He didn't use the internet from his apartment for any of these activities. Instead he engaged in war driving, which was driving around until he found an unsecured internet connection, joining the network, and working from his car. Life as Timothy Freeman kept Hamilton satisfied for just over a year. Just after his twenty-third birthday he realized he needed a change.

His first investor scam took place in Florida. His new name was Albert Grove and his appearance was so altered that he doubted his parents would have recognized him had they still been alive. The adrenaline rush he felt when, after seven months of laying the groundwork, he disappeared with just over $100,000 was orgasmic. He routed the money through the various bank accounts he had set up, listed the money as income from foreign investments, and paid the taxes. He chose Dallas, Texas as his new temporary home, chose the name Harold Browning, and began planning his next job.

It was while he was living in Dallas that he learned of Rachel Whitman. Rachel's husband and two children had been killed in a horrifying accident eighteen months earlier when the family had been vacationing in Maui. Rachel, five months pregnant at the time, had declined to go on a helicopter tour of the island with her family. The helicopter had crashed and the family had perished. The stress brought on early labor and the infant could not be saved. To avoid the horrific publicity the tour company had provided a multimillion dollar settlement. Rachel was young, vulnerable, and rich.

Harold Browning made it his mission to learn everything about the young widow. She was twenty-eight years old; four years his senior. She lived in a house in Coppell, a suburb of Dallas located in the northwest corner of Dallas County. Once Harold had her social security number he had entry into her entire life. Her therapist's notes gave him everything he needed. By the time he finished reading them he knew Rachel Whitman as well, or better, than she knew herself. While she was trying to move forward in her life, one thing she had been unable to give up was a daily trip to the coffee shop where she and her husband had met. Harold studied pictures of her late husband

and modeled his disguise after the man. He made himself reminiscent of him, not an exact copy, but enough to hopefully catch Rachel's eye.

On a humid day in early May Harold made his move. He stood in line behind Rachel as she ordered her coffee and bumped her as she turned to walk away from the counter. The coffee spilled and he insisted on replacing it. He ordered an iced mocha latte for himself. Harold despised the drink, but it just happened to be her late husband's favorite. In this simple way he made the acquaintance of Rachel Whitman. Much to his surprise, Harold found he enjoyed his time with Rachel immensely. She was pretty, intelligent, and easy to be around. He proposed on Christmas Eve, she accepted, and they were married in a simple ceremony at the local courthouse.

The problem began a few months after their wedding when Rachel announced that she wanted them to have a child. Procreating was not in Harold's life plan and he began to spot flaws in Rachel's appearance and personality that he had not previously noticed. By April he was investigating ways to get rid of her.

66

TRINITY GLASS

Trinity and Loyal woke with the sun. They dressed and walked back out to the side of the shed where Loyal had found the disposable hand warmer. It was sunny now, but snow had fallen through the night and the depression and bootprints were filled in. They returned to the house, started coffee, and discussed their plans for the day.

"I only have one day left," said Trinity. "I think we should concentrate on the storage unit."

"Someone was outside the house last night," Loyal said. "There's no alarm system. I'm not thrilled about leaving it unprotected."

Trinity shrugged, "It's up to you, Loyal. This is your show. I'm just along for the ride."

Loyal stood. "I'll plow the driveway. The weather app says no snow until later this afternoon. Let's spend a few hours at the storage unit and plan on getting back here before the snow and while it is still light."

Trinity nodded. "I'll make some breakfast while you plow."

. . .

Before she started making any food Trinity connected her computer and phone and created a hot spot. Her colleague had responded to her request about the ring. Interestingly, it showed up in an investigation in 2006. There was not an actual picture of the ring, just a drawing which her colleague had attached a picture of. Trinity opened the attachment and compared the drawing to the picture Loyal had. To her they looked identical. She returned to the email and continued reading. The ring was evidence in an investigation into a series of investment scams starting in Florida in 2003. The MO was always the same. A man hired a real estate lawyer to set up a few minor deals for him. He won the lawyer's trust, then offered information on some type of investment opportunity. The lawyer attracted a few other investors, they deposited their money, and it disappeared with the mystery man. No pictures of the man existed. Trinity's colleague had attached copies of police sketches. She opened the attachments and flipped through them. The man looked completely different every time. His eyes, hair, nose, and chin showed no similarities. His weight was always estimated differently. The only similarity was the height, which his victims estimated to be between 5'9" and 5'10".

Trinity sent a quick email thanking her colleague and providing as much information as she had about the Maynard Lily investment scam. She included his phone and email and suggested her colleague reach out to him. She was just starting the scrambled eggs when Loyal walked back in the house. She filled him in on what she had learned while they ate.

67

DEAN HAMILTON

Hamilton slept in longer than he had planned. His dreams had been filled with images of his late wife, Rachel. He hadn't thought about her since he had killed her and was troubled that she had invaded his sleep. He lay under the warm covers for nearly half an hour after he woke and replayed his last time with her in his mind.

They had been in Wyoming. Pretending to capitulate to her requests for a child, Hamilton had rented a luxury cabin for the two of them on the outskirts of the Medicine Bow-Routt National forest. The two story cabin was located at the end of a three mile dirt road. Hamilton, still using the name Harold Browning, flew out to Wyoming before renting the cabin. He told Rachel he wanted to make sure it was perfect. This was partially true. He also was using this trip to purchase a used truck from an older man in Laramie. He drove the truck to a spot about a mile from the cabin and hid it in the woods. He hitch-hiked back to Laramie, retrieved his rental vehicle, and flew home to tell Rachel the spot was perfect. They had arrived on a beautiful day in early May. Unfortunately for Rachel, she never had the opportunity to enjoy the cabin. Hamilton strangled her within minutes of arriving. He dug a deep grave in the softening spring soil and dumped her unceremoniously into it. He covered her in dirt, spent two days enjoying the cabin's amenities, then hiked to his truck and drove away. He didn't have to return to Dallas to empty the bank accounts. He simply moved the money in the same way he had in Florida. When he drove into the small mountain town of Taos a week later he was Dean Hamilton.

Hamilton rolled out of bed just after 8:00. He took a long, hot shower and let the images of Rachel wash out of his mind. He replaced them with images of the woman he had seen with Loyal Truesdale. Hamilton dried and dressed in soft gray jeans and a 100% Icelandic wool black and gray sweater. He slipped a pair of cashmere and suede moccasin slippers onto his feet and walked to the kitchen to prepare some coffee. Ten minutes later, steaming mug in his left hand, Hamilton sat down at his computer. He had reasoned, while in the shower, that the woman with Truesdale had flown into Albuquerque from somewhere else. He hacked into the Albuquerque airport's TSA videos and began searching. He knew Truesdale's arrival date and began there. If she had arrived by plane Hamilton would be able top find an image of her. Once he had that he planned to learn everything about the woman.

68

TRINITY GLASS

Trinity and Loyal drove to the storage unit together in his rental truck. They unlocked the unit and began working in much the same way they had the previous day. Trinity went to the back of the unit and Loyal stayed towards the front. After about an hour had passed Loyal approached Trinity.

"I'm thinking I should talk to Francine about the financials," he said. "I'm finding stocks and investments that I need to understand more about. You want to go to her office with me?"

Trinity looked up from the box she was sorting through.

"I think I'll stay here and keep working," she said.

Loyal nodded, "I'll be back as soon as I can."

Trinity pushed aside the box she had just finished looking through. It had contained more books and maps about New Mexico. She had paged through all the books, hoping against hope that a letter or note would fall out. The only thing of interest that she had found was a picture tucked inside a book about the history of Taos. It was a black and white picture of a man she assumed was Walker. His face was not clearly visible. He was wearing a flight suit and a high altitude flight helmet and carrying parachuting gear. She tucked it in her pocket to show Loyal later. She felt strongly that there had to be some clues in this unit explaining why Walker had abandoned the family he loved. She stood, stretched, then sat back down on the cold cement floor. She pulled another box toward her. It was caked with dust and tied closed with twine. Trinity rose, walked to the roll top desk and located a pair of scissors. She returned to the box, knelt beside it, cut the twine, and opened it up.

The box was filled with twenty dollar bills. Not the current iteration, but the old fashioned style with the small oval portrait of Andrew Jackson in the center. The Federal Reserve designation, in the case of the bill Trinity had picked up and held in her hand an **L**, was printed to Jackson's left. Trinity looked at the date on the bill she held; 1969. She looked at the serial number of the top bill. 36246726A. The serial numbers of the bills below the top one were in sequential order. Trinity spent the next ten minutes counting the twenty dollar bills. There were 450 in all. She pulled her phone out of her pocket and used the calculator to do the math. 450 multiplied by 20 came to $9,000. She rocked back on her heels and thought about this for a minute. A thought crossed her mind, but she pushed it away. It couldn't be possible. She slipped her phone and a small stack of twenties back into her jacket pocket. She closed the box and set it aside to share with Loyal when he returned.

69

PATRICK O'KEEFE

Just after 10:00 the warrant was approved. Pat called Dr. Patek's office and made an appointment to meet with the doctor at 12:30. He called Hammond's extension. The detective answered on the second ring.

"We've got the warrant for the pacemaker information," Pat said. "I have an appointment with Dr. Patek at Scripps at 12:30."

"I'll meet you there," said Hammond.

Pat disconnected without saying anything further. He spent the next two hours working on various cases. At noon he closed everything up and headed to Scripps.

Pat and Hammond met up in the lobby and took the elevator to Doctor Patek's office which was located on the third floor. Hammond identified himself and Pat to the receptionist. Her expression was less than friendly as she picked up the phone extension and called the doctor. A moment later a side door opened and a slim dark man wearing a suit and tie leaned out.

"Come on in detectives," he said as he held the door for

them. Hammond and Pat followed the doctor into his office. He indicated the visitor chairs fronting his desk and took his place behind it. He folded his hands together on the desk and leaned towards them.

"I have to tell you I am unhappy about this situation," he said. "A patient's information should be private. I do understand,' he added, "that I have no choice but to cooperate with you. I just want it on record that I disagree with this process."

"This is a potential murder, doctor," Hammond said. "I would think that overrides patient privacy. The data has the potential to either exonerate or implicate. We won't know which way it will go until we see what you have."

Dr. Patek nodded, then leaned back. He picked up a stack of papers from his desk.

"Everything you requested is here," he said. "I suppose you have some questions for me?"

Pat leaned forward, "Just one really," he said. "Was Frederick Young sleeping during the four hour window the warrant specified?"

70

WALKER TRUESDALE - NOVEMBER 1971

Jameson called Walker just after 1:00. It was a Thursday and Walker was at work. His boss's secretary took the call, placed Jameson on hold, and tracked Walker down.

"This better be good Jameson," he said as he picked up the receiver, "you know I don't like to be called at work."

"I need to meet with you Walker," Jameson said. "As soon as possible." He paused and when Walker didn't fill the silence he added, "It is important Walker, please."

"Are you in trouble?" Walker asked.

"Yes," said Jameson, "and it is big."

Walker left work early and they met at the newly opened Hernandez Hideaway, a Mexican restaurant located just above Lake Hodges. When Walker walked in he saw his brother alone at a table in the back of the restaurant. He sat with his hands clasped in front of him. His shoulders were hunched. Walker made his way over to the table and sat. When Jameson looked up Walker saw that his eyes were bloodshot and had dark circles beneath them. Jameson's usually perfectly combed hair was mussed, his clothing wrinkled.

"You on drugs?" Walker asked.

Jameson shook his head. He opened his mouth to speak just as the waitress appeared at their table. She set menus, chips, and salsa on their table and asked if they wanted anything to drink.

"Just water please," said Walker.

"I need something stronger," said Jameson. "A shot of tequila and a margarita on the rocks, no salt."

The waitress nodded and walked away.

"I'm in deep to Marco Barrossa," said Jameson. "He wants his money and I don't have it."

Walker sighed. "You need another thousand? I can probably scrape that together." He looked directly into Jameson's red eyes. "But this is the last time Jameson. You need to get your life together."

Jameson laughed. "I appreciate the offer, Walker, but one thousand won't help. Didn't you hear me? I'm in deep."

"How deep?" asked Walker.

After a brief silence Jameson said, "$170,000."

Walker just stared at his brother.

"I can't have heard that correctly," he said. "What could you have possibly spent that much money on?"

"It doesn't matter now," said Jameson. "What matters is that Barrossa is connected. He's the west coast guy for the mob. Deals with Vegas a lot. He wants his money, Walker. He'll kill me if I don't get it."

"I'm not sure what you think I can do Jameson," said

Walker. "I don't have that kind of money. A bank isn't going to loan an amount like that to me."

"Could you sell part of your property?" asked Jameson.

"Not mine to sell," said Walker. "It all belongs to June and I'm not going to ask her to do that." He paused then added, "Besides the property isn't even worth close to that amount."

The two men were silent for a minute or so. Neither looked directly at the other. Jameson finally broke the silence.

"Please Walker," he said, "I need your help."

"What do you want me to do," said Walker, "steal it?" When Jameson didn't reply Walker said, "You do don't you? You are asking me to risk Rita and Loyal. I won't do that."

"I'm your brother," said Jameson.

"Yeah," said Walker slowly, "Rita is my wife. I chose her Jameson. You are my brother and, frankly, often I feel saddled with you."

Jameson flinched, then leaned forward and said in a fierce, low tone, "You wouldn't even have Rita if it wasn't for me. I took you to that dance. If not for me you'd still be a lonely bachelor in Seattle working on another boring Boeing project." He leaned back in his seat, "Hell, I gave her to you Walker."

The waitress reappeared at the table with their drinks. Jameson shot the tequila, then picked up the margarita and took a long sip.

"Everything okay," the waitress asked. Walker nodded. "You ready to order?" she asked. Walker looked at Jameson but his eyes were focused on his drink.

"A beef taco for each of us," he said.

She nodded and walked away. The silence hung heavy in the air between the brothers. Jameson finished his margarita. Walker sipped his water. The chips remained untouched. Neither spoke until after the waitress had delivered their tacos. Walker was the one who broke the silence.

"I need to think about all this," he said as he stood. He took his wallet out of his pocket and dropped two twenties on the table. "Be careful driving home," Walker said. "Del Dios is dangerous." He started to walk away, then turned back. "Oh, and Jameson," he said, "don't drink the waitress's tip."

71

PATRICK O'KEEFE

Doctor Patek's eyes met Pat's across the desk. Pat couldn't help but notice how large and brown they were. Almost bovine, but far more intelligent. Kindness radiated out of them. The doctor held Pat's eyes for a moment then looked down at the papers on his desk. He picked them up and began flipping through them. He looked up again, glanced at Hammond and again at Pat, then said, "A pacemaker is a small device used to treat some arrhythmias. During an arrhythmia, the heart can beat too fast, too slow, or with an irregular rhythm. Pacemakers send electrical pulses to help your heart beat at a normal rate and rhythm." Pat held up his hand. "We know the basics doctor. If this goes to trial you will have an opportunity to explain the way a pacemaker functions. What we need to know at this point is whether Frederick Young was awake or asleep during that four hour window of time."

The doctor paused again. Pat could read the indecision on the man's face. He was sure this meant that Frederick had not been sleeping, but he needed to hear it directly from the doctor. He glanced at Hammond. The detective was sitting in the chair, arms crossed across his chest, legs splayed in front of him, waiting impatiently. He looked back at the doctor.

"No," Doctor Patek said finally, "there is no way he could have been asleep." He paused then said, "Heart rate and pulse were extremely elevated. He was active."

"Can you describe the level of activity?" Pat asked.

The doctor sighed again. "You've met Mr. Young I assume?"

Pat and Hammond both nodded.

"His fitness level is low." They both nodded again. "Whatever he was doing was quite strenuous. I looked back at the last month's worth of data. This period of time was the most active he has been in thirty days."

Pat and Hammond thanked the doctor for his time. He told them to call if they had any more questions. They assured him that they would, then left the office and walked together to the parking lot.

"Looks like Mr. Young is going to need to come back in to answer a few more questions," said Hammond. "You did great work O'Keefe." He tapped the paperwork he held in his left hand against the palm of his right. "He killed his wife and this is going to nail him."

"We know he was active," said Pat, "but we can't prove what he was doing."

"True," said Hammond, "but he's been caught in a lie, and it's a big one." Hammond held out his right hand. Pat hesitated, then shook it.

"I know you are a friend of Truesdale's and don't like me much," said Hammond. "I appreciate your hard work on this one."

72

DEAN HAMILTON

It took Hamilton several hours but he finally found the mystery woman. Video showed her deplaning two days previously on Tuesday afternoon at 4:36 pm. Her flight had originated in Houston, Texas out of the William P. Hobby Airport. Hamilton had only seen her in profile but recognized her immediately. He captured a still frame from the video. He accessed the dark web and using TOR, the core principle of which is onion routing, hacked the NSA. Hamilton was aware that the NSA had a program called EGOTISTICALGIRAFFE that was designed to break the TOR protocol, but he knew that it only worked if the user of TOR made an error at the beginning or destination of the communication. Hamilton did not make mistakes. He uploaded the image into their facial recognition software program. In moments he received the message

This is restricted information on a confidential identity. You are in violation of federal law.

. . .

Hamilton stared at the words for less than five seconds before reacting. When he did react, it was to log out of the NSA and shut down the string of IP addresses he had used so that his location could not be tracked. If they did try to track the person who had run the woman's picture, they would find an IP address in Dubai. Still, Hamilton was nothing if not careful. He leaned back in his chair and ran his hands over his carefully shaved head. Were the Feds on to him, he wondered. How could they have possibly found him? Surely the woman's appearance could not be a coincidence?

Hamilton logged back into Onstar and checked the location of Truesdale's rental truck. It was in public parking in the historic district of Taos. He spent another hour searching for the woman's identity. He finally found her through the car rental agency, but the only information he got was that her name was T. Glass and she had a Virginia driver's license. This was not good news. Nearly all the different federal agencies were located in Virginia. He thought of as many female T names as he could; Tammy, Tracy, Tanya, Tiffany... the list was endless. He searched social media and found hundreds of T. Glass's, but none were the fire haired woman. Hamilton realized his hands were shaking and his breath was coming in short gasps. Who was she and was she here for him? He briefly considered simply leaving. He could create a new identity and run away; start over somewhere else. This was not in his master plan, however, so Hamilton spent some time considering other options.

Hamilton checked back with Onstar. Truesdale's truck was now parked at Hinds and Hinds storage unit . Realizing this might be his only chance, Hamilton quickly dressed in his Iron-Tuff coveralls and Scarpa Phantom 8000 Mountaineering boots. He pocketed his Kimber and a full face mask cover balaclava. He decided to take his truck with the plow attached. He drove slowly, plow raised, and parked in the same spot as he had the previous night. He double checked that he had everything he needed, pulled the balaclava over his head, and opened the truck door.

73

TRINITY GLASS

Trinity worked her way through a box of vintage Taos t-shirts and sweatshirts. She liked the retro look of them and supposed, like everything else Walker had collected, that they had some value. She set the box toward the front of the unit so she could show it to Loyal. She then returned to the back of the unit and found a dirty black backpack. Its zipper pulls were connected together with a zip tie. She picked up the scissors that still lay on the floor of the storage unit and cut the zip ties. She opened the backpack slowly thinking there might be more money inside it. Instead she found what looked like clothing. She lifted the pieces out one at a time and lay them on the floor. There was a pair of dress pants, a white shirt, a jacket, a narrow tie, and a pair of dark sunglasses. The sunglasses were in pristine shape, the clothing was not. The pants, jacket and shirt all had large rips in them. To Trinity it looked as if some giant cat had attacked the garments. The clothing was obviously old and out of style. The narrow tie reminded Trinity of the 1970's. The white shirt had more than a few blood stains on it. Upon further inspection, Trinity determined that the rips in the clothing appeared to be bloodstained as well. While the stains were clearly visible on the white shirt it was hard to see on the black pants and jacket. After studying each piece, Trinity took a picture of each, then folded everything and replaced it in the backpack. She placed the backpack next to the box of twenties in the rear of the storage unit.

As she was straightening up Trinity heard the growl of Loyal's engine approach the unit then shut down. She walked to the front of the unit to meet him. When he exited the truck she could see that his expression was dark.

"Bad news?" she asked.

"I have the paperwork in the truck. Stocks in excess of $100,000, two bank accounts with over $40,000 each," said Loyal. He ran his hands through his hair. "This may sound crazy but I don't want money, Trinity. I want answers. I want the truth. Francine was supposedly his best friend and even she doesn't know why he left us. Would it have been so hard for him to leave a suicide note?"

Trinity had thought quite a bit about the lack of a suicide note. She was having a hard time reconciling Walker's level of organization and the lack of a note. Still, she remained quiet. Loyal seemed on the verge of a melt down and she did not want to add flames to the already smoldering fire.

Loyal stomped to the rear of the unit then back to the front.

"Where is *my* birthday box?" he asked.

"He had your picture by his bed, Loyal."

"God dammit Trinity," Loyal raged, "can you please stop

defending him? He deserted me when I was eleven, and now he has deserted me again."

"There are lots of clues in this unit, Loyal," Trinity said.

"Okay hot shot agent," Loyal thundered, "then you go ahead and figure it out."

"You have five seconds to apologize for that," Trinity said, her eyes locked on his. She mentally counted down, never breaking eye contact with him. He remained silent. Trinity held out her hand.

"I need your keys," she said.

He held them out to her then turned away.

Trinity exited Hinds and Hinds and turned the truck toward Walker's house. She was hurt and angry. Snowflakes started to fall on the windshield as she drove. She thought abut Loyal in the storage unit and decided to leave him there for a while. He could cool down, literally and figuratively. On the drive to the house she thought about his anger. She knew he wasn't actually angry with her. He was lashing out at anything or anyone who was near him. Still, the man was 59 years old. He should be able to control his temper.

Trinity was just turning off the main road onto the drive leading to Walker's house when her phone rang. She assumed it would be Loyal and was surprised to see the caller was Doug Caldwell. She pulled the truck to the side of the drive and answered.

"Glass," she said.

"Someone hacked NSA and ran a picture of you through

Optic Nerve," Doug said. "IP address from Dubai. You have something going on I should know about?"

"No," said Trinity. "When did this happen Doug?"

"Over an hour ago," said Caldwell. "You told me these days off were personal."

"They are," said Trinity.

"Is Truesdale involved?"

She heard the revulsion in his voice when he said Loyal's last name.

"Not that it is your business," Trinity said, "but, yes he is."

"You are losing focus Glass," said Caldwell, "he's not good for you."

"I'll be back at noon tomorrow," said Trinity. She hung up without saying goodbye.

Trinity sat in the truck, engine idling, and thought about this new nugget of information. It was clear to her that whoever was behind the investor scams was an extraordinarily skilled hacker. There was no other way the money could have disappeared. It baffled her mind that the FBI couldn't trace it. Now someone had accessed a picture of her, from where she wondered, and run it through NSA facial recognition. Another act requiring extraordinary skills. And, again, untraceable. Her thoughts turned to Loyal, alone at the storage unit. Her anger at him dissipated as fast as it had formed. She put the truck in reverse and backed back on to the road. Just as she was accelerating forward movement to her right caught her eye. She turned and saw a snowplow, raised and headed for her. Before she could react the plow hit the truck with force. She tried accelerating with no success. Braking didn't help either. The plow driver, who's face was hidden behind the raised blade, was pushing her truck toward the other side of the road and she was helpless to stop it. Trinity pulled her gun and emptied it into the space slightly above the metal plow. The bullets had no effect. She thought about the drop she was being pushed towards. It was a long way down.

74

DEAN HAMILTON

Hamilton had been stepping out of his truck when he had heard the sound of an engine coming toward him. He had slid back in the truck and watched in disbelief as Loyal Truesdale's rental truck slid by him and turned onto the drive to the house. Immediately upon turning the truck had stopped and sat idling for several minutes. Then, as abruptly as it had stopped, the truck was shifted into reverse and backed back onto the road. Hamilton saw his chance and took it. Raising the snow plow he drove straight into the passenger side of the truck. The driver, Hamilton assumed it was Truesdale, tried to escape but it was futile. Hamilton pushed the truck toward the opposite side of the road which he knew to be a large ravine. He heard the sound of gunfire and smiled. Bullets would be of no help. He pushed until the pressure released, then lowered the plow. The truck was gone. Hamilton slid quickly out of his truck and looked down. The snow was falling heavily now and it was hard to see. Eventually he made out the outline of the truck. He guessed it to be about fifty feet down. It had obviously rolled on the way down and was currently upside down, its wheels in the air. The urge to climb down and check was strong, but Hamilton knew the truck had Onstar and the accident would have been immediately reported. He climbed back into his truck and headed for home.

Hamilton pulled up behind his house and plunged the plow into a large snow drift. He disengaged it from his truck and drove back around to the front. He parked and went inside. He removed the balaclava, the coveralls, and the boots. He stashed his Kimber in the drawer beside his bed and went to the wine cellar to find an appropriate bottle with which to celebrate the elimination of Truesdale and the woman. He couldn't guarantee that they were dead, but he was very confidant that they were out of commission.

75

ANTONIO SHAW

Tony parked in the paid lot and walked slowly toward the lawyer's office. He wanted Dale Walker's file and had no clear plan in mind as to how he was going to get it. So far his luck had not let him down. He was hoping it would continue to fall in his favor. He had noticed a security camera outside the lawyer's office on his previous visit. He pulled the hood of his jacket over his head and angled his face towards the ground. Remembering the bell that had announced his arrival before, he opened the door very slowly, reached his hand up and held the clapper as he eased into the office. Surprisingly, it was empty.

Tony crossed quickly to the desk and stepped behind it. The file drawers were labeled alphabetically. He knelt down and pulled open the bottom file drawer that was labeled **T-Z**. He removed his gloves and slid them in his jacket pocket. His fingers flipped through the tabs quickly, located Dale Walker's file, and removed it from the drawer. He was just about to stand when he heard the lawyer's voice.

"Everything is ready to go Edith," she said, "I just need a few signatures from you."

There were a few seconds of silence then she said, "Sure, I can wait for you. Okay then, see you in a bit."

Staying in his crouched position, Tony duck walked to the right and around the corner of the desk. He heard the lawyers footsteps as she came around the left side of the desk and the squeak of the leather as she sat in her chair. Tony scanned through options in his mind. He knew from the lawyer's side of the conversation that she was going to be waiting for the Edith person to arrive and sign papers. He supposed he could simply stand and run, but surely the lawyer would give chase and create a scene in the courtyard. Then he remembered the ceramic pot on her desk. He closed his eyes and pictured the top of the desk. A few clay figurines, a laptop, and the ceramic pot were all that had been on it. He could hear the lawyer's fingers tapping the keys on the computer. She was humming a tune softly while she worked.

Tony made up his mind. He eased his gloves out of his jacket and silently slid them on. In one swift motion he stood, grabbed the ceramic pot by the rim, and smashed it into the lawyer's right temple. The pot was heavier than Tony had anticipated and surprisingly solid. It made a loud thunk as it connected with the lawyers's head. Her head jerked savagely to the left then came back to center, her chin resting on her chest. Blood leaked out of a sizable cut on her right temple. Tony looked at the ceramic pot in his gloved hand. He couldn't believe it hadn't shattered. He considered whacking her again, but decided against it. She hadn't seen him and Edith was on her way. He simply set the pot back on the desk, pulled the hood over his face, tucked the file into his jacket, and walked away.

76

LOYAL TRUESDALE

Loyal sat at the roll top desk and watched the snow falling outside the storage unit. His thoughts were jumbled. He knew he had been intentionally unkind to Trinity and while he had regretted the words as soon as they escaped his mouth, he had been unable or unwilling to form an apology. He considered calling her, but in the end decided to let her have some space. Surely she wouldn't leave him here for long. He pulled his phone out of his pocket and checked it just to be sure he hadn't missed a call or text from Trinity. The screensaver was a picture of the two of them at Font's Point in Borrego. Peter had taken it of them. They sat on the ground, Loyal's arm around Trinity's shoulder, each holding a travel mug of Irish coffee.

Loyal looked at the picture for a long moment, then tapped the phone icon and called Trinity. Her phone rang six times then went to voicemail. Loyal hung up without leaving a message. As he was re-pocketing the phone it rang. It was a number Loyal didn't recognize, but circumstances as they were, he answered it anyway.

"Mr. Truesdale?" said a man's voice.

"Yes," said Loyal.

"This is Adam Hancock with Hertz car rentals. Are you alright sir? We have received notice from OnStar that your rental vehicle has been in a severe accident."

"What?" said Loyal. "When, where?"

"Are you with the vehicle sir?"

"No," said Loyal, "what are the gps coordinates of the accident?"

"Was the truck stolen sir?" said Hancock. "You are listed as the only authorized driver."

"My wife was driving it," said Loyal. "I didn't expect her to be here. What are the coordinates?"

Sir," began Hancock. Loyal disconnected. He closed and locked the unit then ran to the office of Hinds and Hinds.

Loyal was out of breath when he burst through the office doors.

"I need a vehicle," he said to Dave, the office manager. "I was just notified that my wife has been in a car accident."

Dave looked up. "Who notified you?"

"OnStar called the rental company," Loyal said impatiently. "Do you have something I can borrow?"

"Akome runs the thrift shop next door and is always monitoring first responders," said Dave, "let's go see if he heard anything."

Dave and Loyal walked next door. Akome, an older Taos Pueblo native, was sitting behind his register, the shop was empty of customers.

"You hear anything on the scanner recently?" Dave asked.

"Yeah," said Akome, "about fifteen minutes ago. Two things. A single truck off the road just outside of town and an unresponsive woman on Scheurich Lane."

"I need to get to the car accident," said Loyal.

"They already got the woman out," said Akome. "Transporting her to Holy Cross ER." He looked at Loyal. "It's less than ten minutes from here. You need a ride?"

Akome's truck was a beat up old Ford. Not much to look at, but the engine started on the first try and sounded strong. The two men drove in silence until they pulled up in front of the ER. The hospital was a single story and built in a typically Southwestern style. To Loyal it looked more like a museum or art gallery from the outside.

"You want me to wait with you?" Akome asked.

Loyal shook his head. "Thanks," he said, "but we might be here for a while."

Akome nodded then pulled an old receipt from the map pocket and jotted down his number.

"If you need a ride back home give me a ring," he said. "I'll be at the thrift shop for a few more hours."

Loyal reached across the truck and shook Akome's hand, then he slid out of the truck, ran through the falling snow, and entered the ER.

77

PATRICK O'KEEFE

Rather than heading back to the Sheriff's Station, Pat decided to call it a day and head home. It was nearly two o'clock and he could put in a few hours from home. He pulled into the driveway a few minutes before three and was glad to see Olive's minivan parked there. He parked beside her and slid out of the car. He could hear laughter coming from the backyard. He entered the house, dropped his keys and both his personal and work phones on the kitchen counter, then headed outside to his family.

Olive was pushing Sullivan and Piper on the swing set. Ava was in a sling across her chest. When Sullivan saw Pat he jumped off his swing and ran to him. Pat lifted his son in the air then pulled him in close for a hug. Piper managed to squirm off her swing and ran to Pat as well. He knelt down, gathered her up, and stood with both kids in his arms. Olive approached from the side and gave him as much of a hug as she could manage.

"You are home early," she said.

"Yeah," said Pat, "I was craving some family time."

The kids scrambled out of their father's arms and ran back to the swings. Sullivan climbed back on his swing while Piper stood with arms outstretched waiting for parental assistance which Pat was only to happy to provide.

"Something happen today?" asked Olive once the kids were swinging again.

"Met with the doctor who installed the pacemaker in our arson case." Pat said. "It's looking more and more like the husband is guilty at least of the arson, most likely more." He turned toward Olive. "I can't understand it Olive. What happens to make a person go from loving to hating, from nurturing to killing?"

"I don't have an answer for that Pat,"said Olive.

He shook his head, "Me neither," he said.

They stayed outside for nearly an hour playing with the kids and talking about happier subjects. Once they were back inside Olive suggested Pat shower while she made dinner. He happily agreed.

78

LOYAL TRUESDALE

Loyal cooled his heels in the waiting room for nearly an hour before he was allowed to see Trinity. He had continued to refer to himself as Trinity's husband hoping it would speed up the process, to no avail. He sat in the hard plastic chair in the nearly empty waiting room and tried not to imagine the worst. Finally a nurse approached him.

"Mr. Truesdale," he said, "you can see her now." He led Loyal through a series of locked doors, opening them with the ID badge attached to his scrubs. He stopped in front of an open door and held his hand out.

"She's in there," he said.

Loyal entered the room and stopped. Trinity lay in the hospital bed. She was wearing a gown and had a sheet pulled up to her chest. Her eyes were closed. Loyal approached quietly. The first thing he noticed were the stitches on her forehead. They began about an inch above her right eyebrow and tracked to the right across her forehead ending at her temple. They were angry and black, a stark contrast to Trinity's pale skin. As he looked at her more closely he saw that her left arm was immobilized in a light blue sling. She must have sensed his presence because Trinity slowly opened her eyes. They looked at each other in silence for about thirty seconds before Loyal said, "I know my five seconds were up a long time ago, but I'd like to apologize."

Trinity gave a small sigh. "I guess it is better late than never."

Loyal pulled the visitor's chair as close to the bed as he could and grasped her right hand in his.

"I'm so sorry Trinity," he said. "It's my fault you are lying here."

Trinity attempted to shift a bit. Loyal registered the pain that flashed across her face.

"I didn't crash, Loyal," she said, "I was pushed off the road. If you had been with me we would both be laying here, or worse."

Loyal attempted to keep his face impassive so that she would not see the rage he felt inside.

"What happened?" he asked.

"I was heading to your dad's house but I got a call from Caldwell just as I turned onto the drive. I backed out to go back to the storage unit to tell you about the call and a snowplow came at me from the passenger side. I couldn't stop it Loyal. I emptied my gun but I didn't stand a chance. It pushed me right off the edge."

Loyal released her hand and stood.

"It's that damn ring," he said. "First Arnie and now you."

"Caldwell called to tell me that someone had hacked NSA

and run a picture of me through facial recognition," Trinity said. "It triggered an alarm system and notified Caldwell. He called me." She paused, then added, "You have stirred things up by asking about the ring. It has to be the guy you call Damien Sallwell, and his computer skills must be off the charts."

"We need to get you out of here," said Loyal.

"Already done," said Trinity. "Caldwell reached out to Rodger Stuart. He's flying a smaller plane out of McClellan-Palomar Airport in a few hours. The airport here in Taos can handle smaller private planes, just not big commercial ones." Trinity patted the bed with her right hand. Loyal returned to the visitor chair, sat, and held her hand in his.

"You need back up Loyal," she said. "Call O'Keefe. Have him meet Rodger at the airport. He'll fly him out here."

Loyal opened his mouth to object but Trinity gripped his hand tightly.

"Please Loyal," she said, "call O'Keefe." She paused then added, "Do it for me."

79

PATRICK O'KEEFE

Pat was just stepping out of the bathroom, a towel wrapped loosely around his waist, when he heard his personal cell phone ring. He reversed course and walked towards the kitchen rather than the bedroom. He was just about to round the corner when he heard Olive say, "Hello Loyal."

There was a few seconds of silence then she said, "He's just getting out of the shower. I'lll take the phone to him."

Pat heard her move in his direction. He stepped forward to meet her, his hand extended for the phone. He froze at Olive's next words.

"How are you feeling after the other night?" Olive came around the corner and stopped in her tracks. Her eyes met Pat's. "When you went out to that dive bar with Pat?" she said. Olive kept her eyes firmly fixed on Pat's as she nodded and said, "Great, glad to hear that. You take care Loyal, here's Pat." She handed Pat the phone and walked back into the kitchen.

. . .

"Hey Loyal," said Pat.

"I hope I didn't mess things up for you Pat. I wasn't sure what Olive was talking about, but I tried to play it off."

"Its ok Loyal," said Pat, "don't worry about it." He paused then added, "What's up?"

"Can you come to Taos Pat?" said Loyal.

"Taos, New Mexico?" Pat asked.

"Yes," said Loyal, "I could really use your help."

"With what?"

"I don't have time to get into it right now," said Loyal. "There's a plane at Western Flight at Palomar Airport. You need to get there within the hour. Rodger Stuart will fly you out here."

"Isn't that the guy who was flying Agent Glass around last summer?" asked Pat.

"Yes," said Loyal. "He's coming to get her and is willing to let you catch a ride. Please Pat, I really need your help."

"I'll try to clear it with Olive and Captain Williams," said Pat. "I'll get back to you."

"Thanks man," said Loyal as Pat disconnected.

Pat took a minute to organize his thoughts before following Olive into the kitchen. She wasn't there. He found her in the living room. She stood facing the sliding glass doors. Her posture was rigid. Pat walked up and stood beside her. He remained silent, waiting to hear what she had to say. Finally she spoke.

"He tried to cover it up but I could tell he didn't know what I was talking about. He wasn't with you that night was he?"

"No," said Pat.

"Who was?"

"No one," said Pat. "I was by myself. I was embarrassed Olive, I didn't know what you would think if you knew I got that wasted all by myself."

"Why did you?"

"Its this case I've been working. The one I was talking about earlier. I can't wrap my head around someone who loved another person enough to marry her killing her to save a few bucks on alimony. Its messing with my head."

"Those people aren't us Pat."

"I know," Pat let out a deep sigh, "but looking at the pictures of them from two years ago they could have been." He finally turned toward his wife and grasped her hands in his.

"I'm sorry Olive, I never should have lied to you. I love you."

"I love you too," she said. Pat could hear the sincerity behind her words but there was no mistaking the disappointment in her eyes.

80

WALKER TRUESDALE - NOVEMBER 20, 1971

Rita stood, her back against the kitchen counter, and her arms crossed across her chest. Walker stood opposite her. He had his hands in the pockets of his faded blue jeans. It was the Saturday before Thanksgiving and he had just informed Rita that he was leaving the next day on a week long hunting trip in Oregon. This information had not been well received by his wife. The tidbit he had offered up next, however, was what had put her through the roof.

"You are telling me that you are leaving your family at Thanksgiving to take your brother hunting in Oregon?" she said for the second time.

Walker nodded.

"Why?" asked Rita. "Why at Thanksgiving and why all the way to Oregon? There are plenty of places closer than that to go hunting."

"He's in a bad place Rita," said Walker. "I just think getting him away from everything and spending some one on one time with him is important."

"Jameson is trouble Walker," said Rita, "you know it as well as I do."

Walker nodded, "Yeah," he said, "I do. But he's my brother and I can't turn my back on him." He paused then added, "It's the last time Rita. If this trip doesn't straighten him out then I'm done trying."

Walker spent the afternoon packing his gear into his truck. Dinner was quieter than usual. Rita's disapproval was palpable. Loyal, sensing his mother's mood, was quiet as well. After dinner, when Walker picked up a dish towel to dry the dishes Rita was washing, she shook her head and said she would rather do them herself. When they went to bed she turned her back to him. Walker wrapped his arms around her anyway and was relieved when she allowed it. He drove away as the sun rose the next morning. He gassed up, picked up Jameson, and headed north.

81

LOYAL TRUESDALE

Pat returned Loyal's call within ten minutes. He explained that while neither Olive nor Captain Williams was happy with him at the moment he was leaving for the airport. Loyal thanked him and relayed the information to Trinity. She nodded.

"That makes me feel better about everything," she said.

Loyal reached his hand out and traced the stitches on her forehead gently.

"This is going to leave a scar," he said.

Trinity smiled. "I have a few scars already Loyal, you've seen them all."

Loyal looked at her for a long moment then said,"Akome, the guy from the thrift shop behind Hinds and Hinds' office, offered me a ride. I think I should take him up on that and go get your rental. Then I can drive you to the airport and bring Pat back with me."

Trinity nodded her agreement. Loyal could see the exhaustion in her eyes.

"Try and sleep," he said. He leaned down and kissed the

undamaged side of her forehead, then stood up and walked out.

Akome answered on the second ring and was more than happy to give Loyal a ride. He arrived at the ER in just under fifteen minutes. On the drive to Walker's house Loyal explained about the accident and Trinity's condition. He left out the part about the snow plow. Akome dropped him in front of Walker's house. The snow had stopped falling and the bitterly cold air stung Loyal's cheeks as he walked up the front steps. Loyal entered the house and grabbed Trinity's bag from the bedroom and her keys off the counter. He slid into her rental and began the drive back to the hospital. As he was driving he realized why the street name Akome had mentioned in regard to the unresponsive woman had rung a bell. Francine's office was located on Scheurich Lane.

When his progress to the hospital was paused by a red light Loyal called Holy Cross and asked if Francine Blackwater was a patient there. The woman confirmed that she was but would give no more information than that. When she asked his name Loyal disconnected. He parked in visitor's parking, entered the hospital and walked past reception to the bank of elevators. The doors opened and a Taos police officer stepped out. Loyal briefly considered asking him about Francine, but instead entered the elevator car and pressed the button for the third floor. When he entered Trinity's room she was sitting in the bed. In her right hand she held her gun.

82

TRINITY GLASS

Trinity saw Loyal's eyes widen as he stepped into her room.

"Caldwell pulled some strings," she said. "An officer just dropped this off to me. They found it in the truck." She pointed to her bedside table. Loyal recognized his keys and a manilla envelope from Francine containing copies of his father's file. "Here are your keys and the file from Francine," Trinity said. "I asked him to have the officer grab them as well."

Loyal crossed the room and sat in the chair beside her bed. He set her bag on the floor beside him.

"The man has horsepower," he said, "I'd think the detectives would want to hang on to that gun."

"It's unloaded," said Trinity, "but at least I have it."

Loyal gestured at her bag. "I brought your things."

"Thanks," said Trinity, "I was dreading putting on the clothes I was wearing before the crash." She gestured at a white plastic bag at the foot of the bed. "They are in there."

. . .

Loyal leaned forward in his chair, his elbows on his knees and his face nearer to Trinity.

"Francine Blackwater has been admitted to the hospital Trinity," he said. "Do you think you can ask Caldwell to work his magic again and get some information on why she's here and what her condition is?"

Trinity frowned. "He holds every favor he does for me over my head Loyal," she said. "And if it is a favor for you he'll expect double in return."

Loyal nodded and leaned back in his chair. The room was silent for a long moment. Eventually Trinity gave a deep sigh and pulled out her phone. When Caldwell answered she asked if he could get information about the condition of a Holy Cross patient named Francine Blackwater. Caldwell agreed but Trinity could tell by the tone of his voice that the man was losing patience with her.

Less than ten minutes later a doctor stepped into her room. He was tall and lean and his thinning gray hair looked as if he had been running his hands through it. He wore round wire frame glasses and carried a clipboard in his hand. His expression was grim.

"I've been instructed to give you information about one of my patients," he said, "and I'm not happy about it. HIPPA laws exist for a reason." Without waiting for a response from either of them he lifted the clipboard so that he could see it and continued. "Francine Blackwater was attacked in her office this afternoon and suffered a major trauma to her head. She is in intensive care in an induced coma. A bone flap has been removed from her head to allow for swelling of her brain."

. . .

Trinity's eyes met Loyal's. She knew he had to be thinking about Arnie Crenshaw and the similarities in the injuries.

"What are her chances?" asked Loyal.

The doctor lowered the clipboard and looked at Loyal. "Right now it is not looking good. If she makes it through the night I'd say 50/50. Each day that she survives will increase her odds." The doctor reached in the pocket of his white coat and handed Loyal a business card. "Call me tomorrow and I'll give you an update."

Trinity watched as Loyal accepted the card. "I know telling us goes against what you believe," he said, "but Francine is a close family friend." Loyal held out his right hand and after a brief pause the doctor reached out and shook it. He turned and left the room without saying anything further.

83

WALKER TRUESDALE - NOVEMBER 28, 1971

Walker dropped Jameson off exactly seven days after he had picked him up. They pulled up to his granny flat in Rancho Santa Fe just before three o'clock on Sunday afternoon. Walker engaged the parking brake and shifted the truck into neutral but left the engine idling. He reached behind the driver's seat and brought out a backpack.

"I risked my wife and son to help you Jameson," he said, his voice tight with emotion. "I'm done. I don't want to see your face or hear your voice again." He handed the backpack to Jameson who was watching him in stunned silence. "Pay off Barrossa. Make up a story about how you got the money and leave me out of it. Leave town Jameson." He paused then added, "If I ever find out you told Barrossa I was involved in this I'll kill you myself."

Jameson gave Walker a small nod then slid out of the truck without saying a word.

. . .

The driveway was empty when Walker reached his home in Fallbrook. He parked, slid out of the truck, and entered the house. He called out to Rita, Loyal, and June but received no reply. He returned to his truck for his gear bag, then walked to the garage. He opened his gun safe and returned his guns to their proper places. He pulled a small backpack and a cardboard box tied with twine out of his gear bag and placed them on the floor of the safe. The backpack was intended to serve as a reminder of all he had risked to get the money for his brother. The box was intended to aid in escape in case what he had done ever caught up with him.

Walker returned to the house and took a long shower. He dried, wrapped a towel around his waist, and stood in front of a full length mirror in his bedroom to assess the damage. His arms, legs, and torso were covered with scratches and cuts. The deepest cut was on the inside of his right forearm. It was long, stretching from about an inch above his wrist nearly to the crook of his elbow. He had used butterfly bandages to close it. Looking at it now he realized it had probably needed stitches. It was sure to leave a nasty scar. Walker heard a sudden intake of air behind him. He straightened and turned. Rita was standing just inside the bedroom door, her right hand pressed against her mouth, her eyes wide.

"What happened to you," she asked as she lowered her hand and crossed the room to him.

"I'm okay Rita," he said. "I fell into a deep ravine on Thursday. Most of the wounds are superficial."

She reached out and traced her finger down the cut on his forearm.

"This looks pretty bad Walker," she said looking up at him. It was then that he noticed her red rimmed eyes.

"You've been crying," he said.

"It's my mom, Walker," she said. "She started feeling bad on Thanksgiving Day. She was tired and achy and developing a deep cough. By Friday she was having a hard time breathing. She has pneumonia Walker, she's been in the hospital since Friday."

Walker pulled Rita into him and wrapped his arms around her. Her face was against his bare chest and he could feel the wetness and warmth of her tears.

"She's on oxygen Walker," she said. Her words were muffled but he was able to make out the next six that slipped out of her mouth. "I don't think she's coming home."

84

TRINITY GLASS

Trinity left the hospital against the advice of the doctor treating her. She dressed in fresh clothes, allowed herself to be wheeled to the door, then followed Loyal across the parking lot to the Tahoe. He had wanted her to wait at the door so that he could pick her up but she had declined. She did allow him to carry her luggage and the plastic hospital bag containing her belongings and to help her into the passenger seat. It was nearly 7:00. The night sky was black, the stars visible for the first time in days. Loyal drove in silence. Trinity was sure his mind was on Francine Blackwater. When he finally spoke he confirmed her assumption.

"There has to be more than one person," he said with a quick glance at her. "You and Francine were attacked within minutes of each other."

Trinity nodded. "I've been thinking about that as well. The timing suggests Sallwell has an accomplice, but that goes against the little we know about the man. Everything we have learned points to him working alone." She paused, then added, "And why target Francine?"

"To get information about me?" Loyal suggested.

"Seems unlikely," said Trinity, "with his computer skills he should already know everything about you. Attacking her makes no sense. Could be the attacks are unrelated Loyal."

They drove in silence for a few minutes then Trinity said, "I found a few interesting things in the storage unit today."

Loyal glanced at her again. She lifted the plastic hospital bag and reached inside. She removed her jacket and reached in the pocket. When her hand emerged she held the picture of the paratrooper. She set it in the cupholder. Loyal lifted it and looked at it for a brief moment then replaced it.

"I never knew my Dad was in the military," he said. "Just another damn secret he never shared."

"I found that," she said, "and an old dusty box tied with twine. It was filled with old twenties. The series was 1969. There was also an old backpack. It had a suit and a pair of sunglasses in it. The clothes were torn and bloodstained."

When Loyal said nothing she added, "The box and backpack are in the very back of the unit. I think you should concentrate on the older stuff, Loyal. You might learn something valuable."

Loyal ran his left hand through his hair. "I feel like just throwing a match on everything, Trinity. I'm not sure I really want to know what happened with my dad."

Loyal exited Highway 64 and parked beside Taos Aviation Services. He unstrapped his seatbelt and reached out with his left hand to open his door. Trinity reached across her body with her right hand and placed it on his right forearm.

"Wait one minute Loyal," she said.

He turned toward her.

"We need to take a break," she said. "You need to take some time to work out what you are feeling about your dad."

Loyal's eyes widened. "My dad doesn't have anything to do with us, Trinity," he said.

"Yeah, he does," she said. "It is affecting our relationship. You need to work it out." Trinity kept her gaze firmly on Loyal. It was painful to see the hurt in his eyes. She felt her own eyes fill with tears and attempted to blink them back. One escaped her left eye and trickled slowly down her cheek.

She lifted her hand from his arm, turned, and opened the door. A gust of frigid wind blew in. Trinity slid out, turned, and saw that Loyal was exiting the vehicle as well. He carried her bags across the tarmac to the waiting plane. The stairs descended and O'Keefe and Rodger stepped out. Trinity saw the expression of concern on Rodger's face when he saw her injuries and was grateful that he said nothing. He simply took her bags from Loyal and walked back up the stairs. O'Keefe raised a hand in greeting but remained silent as well.

"Will you at least text me when you land?" asked Loyal. Trinity turned to look at him. He looked as sad as she felt. She said nothing, just shook her head and turned toward the plane.

85

LOYAL TRUESDALE

Pat, seeming to sense Loyal's heartache, remained quiet during the drive to the house despite the fact that he had many questions. Gentle snowflakes began falling as Loyal parked in front of his father's house. He turned toward Pat and said, "Thanks for coming Pat. Come on inside. Let's have some food and I'll fill you in on everything that has happened."

Loyal started fires in both fireplaces and gave Pat a quick tour. He cooked the last frozen meal and they sat at the table to eat. Between bites Loyal told Pat everything that had happened since his arrival in Taos.

They decided to sleep in shifts. Pat slept first. He stretched out on the king sized bed, fully clothed except for his shoes. Loyal fed logs into both fireplaces and settled himself into his father's large chair. He had moved it slightly so that the view of him through the narrow window by the front door was obscured. The shotgun lay in his lap. He was alert but let his mind wander any route it chose. Not surprisingly a memory from years ago rose to the surface. Marco Barrossa had sponsored Loyal in motocross racing for years. One particular race came to Loyal's mind. It had taken place in Ensenada. It was Loyal's third time racing in Baja. It was April and he had just turned eighteen. He was set to graduate from high school and had been accepted at SDSU where he was planning on majoring in criminal justice. It had rained through the night and the race course was a muddy mess. Loyal got the hole shot and led the entire race. It was his first win in Mexico. Marco's words of congratulation came to Loyal now. "Too bad your dad isn't here," he had said. "He'd be proud."

Loyal fed the fires again at 3:00, then woke Pat. He stretched out on the bed in the same way Pat had, fully clothed with the exception of shoes. He dropped into sleep quickly and dreamed of Trinity.

86

ANTONIO SHAW

Tony was obsessing over the possibility that the old man had kept a journal somewhere. After his visit to the attorney he had returned to his Airbnb on Cavalry Road and hidden out for the remainder of the day. As evening approached he drove to the hardware store and purchased a five gallon gas container, some shop rags, a bolt cutter, and some twine. He stopped at the gas station, filled the container, and purchased a six pack of Corona. He drove back to the Airbnb and brought everything inside. He opened two Corona bottles and drained the beer into the sink. He refilled the bottles with gas and stuffed a shop rag in the mouth of each bottle. He wrapped the bottles with washcloths and secured them with twine, then placed them carefully in the camelback backpack he used when he was skiing.

Tony dressed in black jeans, black sweatshirt, and black tennis shoes. He rummaged through his skiing apparel until he found the black face mask he wore on frigid days. He placed the mask, along with a disposable lighter, into the pocket of his black jacket and slipped the camelback backpack over his shoulders. He left his Airbnb on foot and walked down Cavalry Drive. It was snowing again which suited his purposes. The one mile walk from the Airbnb to the back side of the fencing surrounding Hinds and Hinds took him just under fifteen minutes. He walked casually to the rear of Smith's Food and Drug, slipped through an unfenced backyard of a home, climbed the fence, and dropped onto the storage unit property.

Tony was on the property for less than ten minutes. He knew from his time in the office that he was being filmed. He had the face mask on and kept his shoulders hunched. He walked straight to unit 56, removed the bolt cutters from the backpack, and cut the lock. He removed the corona bottles from the backpack, unwrapped the washcloths, and raised the door a few feet. He lit them, and tossed them in. The bottles broke on the concrete floor and ignited. The flames found the cardboard boxes and began to grow. Tony watched the fire expand, the flames hungrily working their way up decades old boxes that were dry and brittle. When he was sure the fire would continue to grow he lowered the door, leaving a few inches open for air flow. He retrieved his bolt cutters, slipped the backpack on, and left the same way he had entered.

87

WALKER TRUESDALE - DECEMBER 4, 1971

June was buried next to her husband eight days after she had been admitted to the hospital. The day was cold and gray. The service at the church had been large. The burial was private. Walker, Rita, and Loyal stood together and watched in silence as the casket was lowered into the grave. All three were heart broken and hurting, but it was Loyal that Walker was most worried about. This was the first time Loyal had experienced the loss of a loved one. He and June had been extremely close and her death had been unexpected and shocking. Loyal had hardly spoken since she had passed. He roamed the property after school and went into his room immediately following dinner. Walker's attempts to engage him in conversation were met with sad silence.

Loyal was not Walker's only concern. He assumed that Jameson had given the money to Barrossa by now and could only hope that his brother had kept Walker's involvement to himself. In truth, Jameson had no idea how Walker had obtained the cash.

Walker had deposited his younger brother at a bed and breakfast in Oregon. He had paid the elderly couple who owned it an extra $200 to keep an eye on his brother. After giving Jameson strict instructions not to leave the property or make any phone calls, Walker had headed out on his own.

Jameson had not reached out to Walker. Walker had considered calling his brother when June had died. The two had enjoyed each other's company in the past and he felt his brother deserved to know. In the end Walker had decided to let it go. He hoped that Jameson had heeded his advice and left town after paying Barrossa.

88

TRINITY GLASS

Rodger landed at William P. Hobby Airport and taxied to the Wilson Air Center. He planned to sleep in one of the executive suites for flight crews provided by the air center and take off again early the next morning. He arranged for an Uber for Trinity and helped her with her bags when it arrived. He gave her a one armed hug, taking care not to jostle her damaged collarbone, and wished her well. Trinity gave him a light kiss on the cheek and thanked him again then slid into the Uber, leaned her head back, and closed her eyes.

She walked into the lobby of the hotel just after 10:00 pm. The night clerk, a young man named Jeremy who Trinity had gotten to know during her time in Houston, looked up when she walked in. His eyes widened when he saw Trinity's injuries.

"Ms. Glass," he said as he came out from behind the counter, "are you ok?"

Trinity nodded. "I was in a car accident in Taos but I'm ok."

"Do you need help up to your room?" Jeremy asked.

Trinity smiled and shook her head. "Thanks Jeremy," she said, "I think I can manage."

"Ok," said Jeremy, "call the desk if you need anything."

Trinity took the elevator to the fourth floor and keyed her way into her room. She dropped her bag and the plastic bag from the hospital on the floor and headed straight to the bathroom. Undressing and showering proved to be quite difficult and painful but she managed it. An hour later she was dressed in loose pajamas and sitting at the small dining table in her room. Her hair was damp and uncombed. She held her phone in her right hand and was scrolling through pictures of herself and Loyal. Telling him they needed to take a break had been hard. She was tempted to call him now and take it back but she truly did believe he needed time to examine his feelings for his father. With a sigh she set the phone down, stood, and walked to her bed.

89

LOYAL TRUESDALE

Loyal's phone woke him just after 6:00. He lifted it off the nightstand and looked at the caller ID. It was a local number. Fearing the worst regarding Francine, he answered.

"Mr. Truesdale," said a male voice, "this is Dave from Hinds and Hinds. I'm sorry to tell you this, but there was a fire in your storage unit last night."

"What?" said Loyal.

"It appears to have been intentionally set. The lock was cut and it smells heavily of gasoline. A neighbor smelled the smoke and called it in. The fire department is here now."

Loyal swung his legs off the edge of the bed and stood.

"How bad is it?" he asked.

"Complete destruction," said Dave, "there's nothing left."

Loyal looked out the window and saw that snow was still falling.

"I'm going to have to plow the drive," he said. "I'll be there as soon as I can."

Loyal found Pat in the kitchen making coffee. He explained about the fire, drank a quick cup of coffee, then went outside to plow the drive. He took his PM9 and the shotgun with him.

90

DEAN HAMILTON

Hamilton woke at 4:45 and rolled out of bed. His sleep had been deep and dreamless, his worries about Loyal Truesdale and the woman finally assuaged. He made coffee and took a mug with him when he sat down at his computer. He found an article about the accident and read it quickly. The information, while sparse, was not what he was hoping for. According to the article there had been only one occupant, a woman, in the truck. She had been transported to Holy Cross.

Hamilton leaned back in his chair and let this information percolate for a bit. He was angry, but realized that calm and logical thinking was called for in this situation. After a moment he leaned forward and hacked into Holy Cross to retrieve T Glass' medical records. In this way he learned her first name was Trinity. According to the notes she had been discharged against the advice of the attending doctor. He had added that she was going to be transported out of Taos by private plane.

Her injuries were listed as a three inch laceration on her forehead and a broken collarbone.

Retiring in Taos was Hamilton's plan and he was not prepared to change it. With his girlfriend injured Truesdale was going to be more determined than ever to find him. Hamilton considered his options and finally decided on the one that made the most sense. He would simply have to kill Loyal Truesdale. He dressed in his coveralls and boots and zipped the Kimber into his pocket. He reattached the plow, cleared his driveway, then plunged it back into the drift behind his house. With his balaclava on the seat beside him, Hamilton drove towards Truesdale's house.

He parked in the stand of trees and walked towards the house in the same manner as he had before. As he was walking along the back of the shed he heard an engine start up. He edged up to the corner of the shed and peeked around. He smiled when he saw that Truesdale was just starting to plow his drive. What perfect luck. He pulled the balaclava onto his head, removed the Kimber from the zippered pocket, and headed for the front door. With Truesdale's back to him he could simply walk into the house and wait. He'd sit in the chair he'd seen Truesdale sitting in. When the former detective returned from plowing Hamilton would simply shoot him and walk away.

91

PATRICK O'KEEFE

Pat was standing in the living room when he heard the front door opening. He watched in stunned silence as a masked man, gun held loosely in his right hand, entered and turned to close the front door. The man turned and their eyes met. In the micro second it took Pat to process what he was seeing he realized that the man's eyes, the only feature he could see, were an unusual shade of pale blue. Beyond that detail Pat noticed nothing else but the gun. Without another thought he simply reacted. He lunged across the space between them and hit the intruder hard. Their bodies slammed backwards and hit the closed front door with force. The masked man, who Pat could tell was fit and strong, pushed off the door and sent their bodies flying roughly to the floor. Pat heard the gun drop from the man's hand and skitter across the floor.

The intruder landed on top of Pat and immediately began raining punches down on him. Pat reached up and pulled the masked man closer to him, then wrapped his right leg around the intruder's left foot. He reached his right arm over the intruder's left and in a burst of power exploded while rotating his body to the right. This movement resulted in Pat being on the top with the intruder beneath him. The two men rolled and grappled, punching and kicking each other. Pat was trying to control the intruder's hands when the man pushed off the ground with speed and agility. He flipped Pat over and sat astride him. Rather than punching, he wrapped his hands around Pat's throat and began to squeeze. Pat punched at his masked face as hard as he could but the hands did not release. Pat felt his arms grow weaker and drop to the floor. He found he was unable to lift them. He looked straight into the stranger's pale blue eyes, but his last coherent image was of Olive and his three young children.

92

LOYAL TRUESDALE

Loyal finished plowing and parked the truck, plow still attached, beside the shed. More snow was predicted, so he figured he would drive Trinity's rental and leave the plow attached and ready for use. Carrying the shotgun loosely in his left hand, he walked up the stairs, crossed the porch, and opened the front door. It took him about two seconds to recognize what he was seeing. A masked man was on top of Pat. He had his hands around Pat's neck and Pat was not moving. There was no way Loyal could take a shot without hurting Pat, so he simply crossed the room and brought the butt of the shotgun down on the intruder's head. The masked man fell off Pat and to the right. Loyal slammed the butt into the man's head another time then turned to Pat. He was laying unmoving on the floor. Handprints were visible on the pale skin of his neck and a large bruise had begun to form beneath his left eye. Loyal knelt, felt his neck for a pulse, and breathed a sigh of relief. He was alive but unconscious.

. . .

Loyal pulled out his phone and dialed 911. He tapped the speaker function and carried the phone with him as he went to the kitchen for some twine. He set the phone on the floor next to the intruder and gave his address and details to the woman who answered while he secured the man's wrists and ankles. He explained that he was a retired detective and that Pat was active duty and both were armed. He considered pulling the balaclava off the intruder, but saw that it was damp where he had hit him and decided to leave it in place. He didn't want blood all over the floor. The front door was still open, so Loyal simply sat down on the floor next to Pat to wait for the police and paramedics.

93

WALKER TRUESDALE - JANUARY 19, 1972

Walker was awakened by the phone ringing. He glanced at the bedside clock and saw that it was 4:12 in the morning. He considered not answering but the insistent ringing was sure to wake the family so he slid out of bed and walked into the kitchen. He lifted the receiver and was sure his voice sounded rough and angry as he said hello.

"Mr. Truesdale?" said a male voice.

"This is he," said Walker.

"My name is Officer Reynolds," said the man, "I'm with the Escondido Police Department. I'm sorry to be the one to deliver this news sir, but your brother Jameson Truesdale was in a car accident on Del Dios Highway a few hours ago." Officer Reynolds paused, then added, "I'm sorry sir, he didn't survive."

The officer gave Walker details about the location of the accident, the yard where Jameson's car would be towed, and the hospital where his body would be located. He explained that the accident had been a single car crash. There was a strong smell of alcohol in the car and they were assuming that Jameson had had too much to drink and failed to negotiate a curve in the road. Walker thanked Officer Reynolds for calling and placed the receiver slowly in the cradle. He took two steps and let his body sink slowly into a kitchen chair. He had been confident that Jameson had left the area and was finding it hard to believe that his brother had stayed. He had been serious when he had told Jameson that he wanted no further contact but had never expected something like this.

Walker dressed quietly so as not to wake Rita, made a pot of coffee, poured a large mug full and spent the next hour walking around the property. Thoughts of Jameson filled his mind. His brother had always needed Walker's help and protection. It began as soon as Jameson learned to walk and had lasted until the very end. Memories and images floated through Walker's inner field of vision. He couldn't begin to count the number of times he had saved Jameson from being beaten up as his younger brother walked home from school. And of course there was the last time he had helped his brother, risking everything in the process.

It was just past 5:30 when Walker stepped back inside his home. The sky was still dark; sunrise nearly ninety minutes away. He rinsed the mug and set it in the sink then walked back into his bedroom and woke Rita. When she heard what had happened her eyes filled with tears. Walker knew the tears were for him and his pain. Rita had not cared for Jameson.

"I need to go to the lot where they towed his car," said Walker. "It is in Escondido."

"Do you want me to come with you?" Rita asked.

Walker shook his head. "I think I need to do this by myself," he said.

He changed into slacks and a button down shirt, kissed his wife, and walked to his truck.

Walker arrived at the tow yard on the northwestern edge of Escondido a little past 7:00. The sign on the gate informed him that the yard opened for business at 8:00. He sat in his truck and closed his eyes. Much to his surprise he fell asleep and was awakened by a tapping on the driver's side window of his truck. A wizened, weather beaten older black man with thick gray hair who was barely tall enough to see into the window peered in at him with a questioning look on his face. Walker opened the door and stepped out.

"Help you?" asked the man.

"I'm here about my brother's car," said Walker. "He was in an accident on Del Dios Highway early this morning. It's a red Porsche 911T."

The old man led Walker to Jameson's car. Walker paused and drew in a long slow breath when he saw it. The front and rear were smashed, as was the windshield. It appeared to Walker that the convertible top had been open. He drew nearer and looked inside. Plant debris and dirt filled the car. The smell of alcohol was still emanating from the car, almost as if the vehicle had been dipped into a vat of it. The old man pointed to a nearly empty bottle of gin behind the driver's seat.

"Don't know how that survived, but it was in the car when they brought it here."

A chill ran down Walker's spine. In that instant he knew this had not been an accident. Jameson abhorred gin. He would never have gotten drunk on it. He thought about Marco Barrossa and the money and wished again that Jameson would have taken his advice to pay up and leave town. Something had gone wrong and Jameson had paid the ultimate price.

94

LOYAL TRUESDALE

Two hours after his initial 911 call Loyal was allowed to leave his house. Pat had regained consciousness after the arrival of the police, paramedics, and the fire department. He had initially refused medical care, but Loyal had convinced him that it would be a good idea to be examined after what he had endured, so he had been transported to Holy Cross. The detective had arrived shortly after the marked unit that had responded to the 911 call. The intruder had no identification on him and had been taken to Holy Cross as well. He would receive medical care there and be placed under arrest. Loyal had explained everything to the detective, starting from Maynard Lily's theft and moving forward through Arnie's accident, the night time visitor, Trinity's accident, and the current situation. The detective listened and took notes, but Loyal wasn't sure how much he believed. Before the detective left Loyal gave him the pictures of Damien Sallwell and his ring. Loyal's phone rang continuously throughout the conversation with the detective and in the end he had simply turned his phone off.

. . .

Once the house was empty Loyal turned his phone on again. He had multiple voicemails from the rental agency urging him to return their call as quickly as possible. Loyal ignored those messages. There was one message from Dave at Hinds and Hinds wondering if Loyal was on his way to see the damaged unit. This call he returned. He explained that he had been unavoidably held up and that he was on his way now. He slipped his belly band and PM 9 around his waist and slid into Trinity's rental. The drive to the storage unit took a bit longer than expected. The snow had stopped and the day was bright and clear. In spite of the freezing temperature the roads were busy.

Loyal drove past the office of Hinds and Hinds and straight to unit number 56. The sliding door was open and crime scene tape was strung across the opening. Loyal parked and slid out. He stood in front of the unit and surveyed the destruction. Dave had told him the truth, it was a total loss. All that remained was a mass of wet ashes. The smell of gasoline hung in the air. Loyal thought about his comment to Trinity before she had flown away the previous evening about throwing a match on everything. Someone else had done it for him. As he stood and stared at the burnt remains Loyal's thoughts drifted back to the months before his father had vanished. Walker had been uncharacteristically moody and short tempered in the months before he had left. Loyal had always attributed this to the deaths of June and Jameson. He wondered now if perhaps it had been something else. He started with the day in January that Jameson had died and mentally worked his way backwards in time. December had passed in a haze of grief. Loyal remembered Walker trying to talk to him about his grandmother's death, but Loyal had been unwilling. He thought about the days leading up to June's death. She had been hospitalized the day after Thanksgiving and had never come back home. He remembered now that Walker had not spent Thanksgiving with the family. He had taken Jameson hunting.

The more he thought about it, the more Loyal wondered if something had happened on that trip. His father had come home with cuts and scrapes all over his body. The worst cut had been on his forearm and had left an angry scar that reached from just above his wrist nearly to his elbow. The only time Walker had been in a good mood after Thanksgiving had been Loyal's birthday. His father had picked him up early from school that day. When they arrived at the house he had presented Loyal with a new motorcycle and the two of them had spent the rest of the day riding around the property. Walker had seemed to be his old self again. Then the next day he had been gone.

Loyal gave his head a small shake. He pulled his phone from his pocket and took a few pictures then slid back into Trinity's rental. He drove back to the office, parked, and went inside. Dave was at his desk and looked up as Loyal entered.

"I saw on the cameras that you already looked at the unit," he said.

"Total loss," said Loyal, "just like you said."

"Definitely arson," said Dave. "I made a copy of the footage before the police confiscated it as evidence, but it doesn't tell us much."

He waved Loyal over and turned his computer so that they both could see the screen. He tapped a few keys and the image from the cameras appeared on the monitor.

"Give it a few seconds," said Dave. "This is footage from a camera opposite your unit."

Loyal watched as a dark figure appeared on the screen. He could tell by the way he moved that it was a man. His shoulders were hunched and his head covered by the hood of his jacket. He walked directly to Loyal's unit, removed a small backpack and knelt in front of the door. Although the footage was grainy and dark, Loyal could see enough to realize the lock was being cut and the door partially opened. The man removed something else from the backpack. There was a spark of light as he lit something, then a brighter flash as he tossed it into the unit. The flames caught quickly and soon the contents were completely engulfed in flames. The man put his backpack back on and lowered the door part way. He turned so that he faced the camera and it was then that Loyal saw he was wearing a face mask. Without a backwards glance he simply walked away.

Dave tapped a few keys and a different view appeared on the screen. A different camera had captured the man climbing the fence and dropping down on the other side.

95

WALKER TRUESDALE - JANUARY 21, 1972

Jameson was laid to rest on a bitterly cold Friday. He was buried at Oak Hill Cemetery in Escondido. Walker was the only attendee. He stood alone, his hands in his jacket pockets and his shoulders hunched against the cold, and watched as the coffin was lowered into the frigid ground. His heart felt as cold as the wind that blew against his face, his soul as dark as the dirt piled next to the grave. He had tried, to no avail, to convince the police that his brother's accident may not have been accidental at all. Drunk driving was the official determination. He watched now as two men, shovels in hand, approached the grave and began to fill it in. The scoops of dirt landed on the coffin with gentle thuds.

Walker heard the sound of a car door being closed, then the sound of footsteps approaching behind him.

"Shame about your brother's accident," a male voice said from just behind his left shoulder.

Walker turned slowly. Marco Barrossa was standing just

behind him. Walker felt a sudden rage and took a step towards the man. It was then that he noticed two more men standing about ten feet behind Barrossa. He stopped his forward movement and said, "I'm not convinced it was an accident."

Barrossa shrugged. "Doesn't matter much, the end result is the same."

The two men stood and looked at each other in silence for a long moment. Barrossa spoke first.

"Your brother owed me a lot of money," he said. "He mention that to you on your hunting trip?"

Walker shook his head but said nothing.

"He gave me some cash a few months ago," said Barrossa, "but it turns out the money's no good. I took some to Vegas over New Year's. Didn't spend too well." He held Walker's eyes with his own. "You know what I'm talking about?"

Walker frowned and shook his head. "Afraid not," he said.

"Under the circumstances I'm considering the debt unpaid," said Barrossa.

"You should have taken that up with my brother," said Walker.

Barrossa smiled but there was no warmth in it. "Oh I did," he said, "believe me. Jameson couldn't tell me where the money came from. I'm confidant he didn't know or he would have told me." Barrossa paused then added, "He never gave you up though."

Walker knew in that moment that Jameson had indeed been murdered. He wanted to rip Barrossa limb from limb but knew if he made a move the two men would kill him where he stood. He had no intention of dying in this cemetery today.

"I'm assuming you are here for a reason," he said.

Barrossa smiled that cold smile again and said, "Yes, actually, I am. You are Jameson's only family. His debt has now become yours. $170,000. You have two months."

Before Walker could open his mouth to dispute this statement Barrossa had turned and walked away.

96

LOYAL TRUESDALE

Loyal left Hinds and Hinds and drove straight to Holy Cross. While he drove he thought abut the things that had been destroyed and the things that had not. The paintings, figurines, and Stella's necklace were all safely stashed at his father's house. Try as he may, Loyal could not come up with a logical reason for someone to burn his father's things. Something Trinity had said was hovering just out of reach. When he reached the hospital he saw that there was a marked unit in front of the entrance. It was parked haphazardly and its lights were flashing. Loyal wondered what else could have possibly happened in Taos today. Just as he pulled into the hospital parking lot he remembered what Trinity had said. She had wanted him to look at something in the storage unit. He searched his memory and came up with it as he was crossing the parking lot to the front door; cash and a torn suit.

O'Keefe had not been admitted to the hospital. He had been examined by a doctor, handed over to the detective for questioning, then released. Loyal found him in the ER waiting room. The finger marks on his neck had deepened in color, as had the bruise beneath his left eye. The bruised area had also swollen considerably which was causing his left eye to squish shut. Loyal approached him and sat beside him.

"How you doing Pat?" he asked.

When he answered Pat's voice was rough and whispery. "Hard to talk and swallow," he said. "They gave me some Tylenol and this cold pack." He held up a thin disposable cold pack that he had been holding in his lap. "Supposed to keep it on my neck but it hurts like hell." He swallowed gingerly then said, "You saved my life, Loyal. I could feel it fading away."

Loyal looked directly into Pat's blue eyes. "You saved mine, Pat," he said. "If you wouldn't have been there he would have attacked me as I walked in." Loyal paused, then added, "I'd like to check on Francine while I'm here if you don't mind waiting a few more minutes."

Pat shook his head, closed his eyes, and leaned back in the chair.

Loyal pulled the doctor's card out of his wallet and placed a call to him. He answered on the fourth ring.

"It's Loyal Truesdale," said Loyal, "I was wondering about Francine Blackwater's condition."

"She survived the night," said the doctor. "She's still in the coma. The swelling in her brain has not subsided. The bone flap has not been replaced."

"Can I see her?" Loyal asked.

"Not yet," said the doctor. "Check in with me daily and if she shows improvement we can reconsider that."

Loyal thanked the doctor and cut the connection. He

turned his attention back to Pat who remained in the same position, his eyes still closed. Loyal patted his arm and said, "What do you want to do Pat?"

Pat opened his eyes and straightened. "I'd like to go home Loyal," he said in his whispery voice. "The guy is in custody now and I'd really like to see my family."

97

DEAN HAMILTON

Hamilton had come to in the ambulance but feigned unconsciousness keeping his eyes closed and his muscles as relaxed as possible. Despite the application of a numbing agent he had felt each stitch used to close the gash in his left temple. The total had been nine. He had determined by their voices that the doctor was a woman and the nurse was a man. They both sounded very young. He was currently in a temporary room in the emergency area of the hospital. He was surprised that he was not handcuffed to the bed. He remembered that the red haired man had been unconscious, but wasn't sure if he had lived or died. The doctor and nurse were discussing his upcoming CT scan when a phone rang. Hamilton listened to the doctor's half of the conversation, which was short and to the point. Her attention was required elsewhere. She instructed the nurse to remain with the patient. Hamilton heard the door click closed, then heard it reopening almost immediately. A male voice said, "Is the patient still unconscious?"

"Yes," replied the nurse.

"If you are going to be here I'd like to grab a coffee."

"Sure officer," said the nurse. "Cafeteria is on the second floor."

Hamilton wasted no time. As soon as he heard the door click closed he opened his eyes a tiny crack. The nurse was standing by his bed, phone in his hands, his thumbs tapping rapidly. Hamilton surged out of the bed, grabbed the startled nurse by the neck, and slammed his head into the wall. The man slumped immediately. Hamilton managed to wrap his arms around the slender man's torso and manhandle him onto the bed. He leaned down and retrieved the nurse's phone from the floor and breathed a small sigh of relief when he saw that the screen was still active. Hamilton went online and ordered an Uber to come to the hospital. He used a credit card with an alternate identity. He was informed that a Subaru Outback driven by Leslie would arrive in 6 minutes. Hamilton stripped the scrubs off the still unconscious nurse then pulled the thin blanket up to the man's chin. He dressed in the scrubs, which were a bit tight and an inch too short, but would serve Hamilton's purposes fine. In the back pocket he found a disposable mask and cap which he put on. He held the nurse's phone in front of him like he was texting and eased out of the room. Nobody even glanced his way as he walked down the hall and out into the cold.

Hamilton leaned against the outer wall, phone in hand, and watched for Leslie and the Subaru. She arrived as promised. He slipped the mask off his face and slid into the back seat, trying to look as casual as possible. He kept the cap on to cover what he was sure were nasty looking stitches. When they pulled into his driveway he asked Leslie if she would be willing, for an extra $200, to pick up his girlfriend in Santa Fe. He had no girlfriend, he simply wanted Leslie far away in case anyone connected the Uber request with his escape. She agreed, so he ordered an Uber for an address in Santa Fe and she accepted. He then turned off the nurse's phone and dropped it on the floor of the car. He went into his house and returned with two crisp $100 bills, which he handed through the driver's side window. He watched Leslie drive away and returned to his house.

Hamilton was unsure if the police knew his identity. He had carried no identification when he went to Truesdale's house, only the Kimber which he had dropped and was now surely in police custody. His hope was that he could someday return to his home in Taos but realized that was likely years away. He spent ten minutes altering his appearance. His first glance in the mirror had shocked him. The stitches were dark against his pale skin and bald head. He chose a dark brown wig that covered the angry wound and used face putty to enlarge his nose and chin. He packed a suitcase with his favorite clothes and picked three bottles of wine from his cellar to take with him. He grabbed a brand new lap top out of his office and loaded everything into his Mandalay 40G motorhome that he kept in a large garage in the corner of his property. He took a final look around his beloved house, locked the doors, and drove away.

98

LOYAL TRUESDALE

Loyal looked up aviation services at Taos Airport and learned that a company called Taos Air had flights out of Taos to four hubs and was pleased to see that Carlsbad happened to be one of them. He booked a seat for Pat on a flight that left at 12:30 pm. It was just past 10:00 am now so they had time to get Pat's things from the house and get back to the airport half an hour before the flight was scheduled to depart. Loyal suggested stopping for some food but Pat did not think he would be able to swallow anything. Loyal had Pat wait in the car while he gathered up his friend's things. He placed a call to Olive while he was in the house and explained what had happened. He gave her the flight information and she promised to be there when Pat landed. Loyal could hear both worry and anger in her voice. He apologized repeatedly. When they hung up he found himself wondering if Olive was going to try to keep Pat away from him. He supposed he couldn't blame her if she did.

. . .

Both Loyal and Pat had been allowed to keep their weapons because neither of them had been discharged. The shotgun, which Loyal had used to bash the intruder's head, was in police custody and would remain so until a determination of self defense had been issued by the District Attorney. Loyal was wearing his PM9 on his waist. Pat's gun, a Glock 22, was with his things. Loyal handed Pat the Glock and set Pat's baggage in the back seat. They arrived at the airport with time to spare.

Loyal remained with Pat until he boarded, then watched from the Tahoe until the plane took off. They had said little to each other while they waited for Pat to board. Loyal had told him about the conversation with Olive and that she would be in Carlsbad to get him when he landed. Other than that they had sat silently, each man lost in his own thoughts. Once the plane was in the air Loyal headed back to the historical district for something to eat. He chose La Cueva Cafe, a small restaurant featuring traditional New Mexican entrees. He ordered two beef tacos and was just digging in when his phone rang. It was a local number so he answered it, thoughts of Francine in his mind. Surprisingly, it was the detective who had come out to his house that morning.

"I have some news for you Mr. Truesdale," he said. "The intruder from your house escaped the hospital this morning. Disappeared into thin air."

Loyal let out a long sigh. "No leads?" he said.

"Nope," said the detective, "he overpowered a nurse while the officer stationed outside his door was getting coffee." The detective paused and then said, "That's being dealt with, but the bigger issue is the guy is on the loose and we don't even have an ID on him yet. You might consider staying in a hotel. I'll let you know when we get him."

99

ANTONIO SHAW

When Tony had returned from setting the storage unit on fire he had been keyed up and anxious. He had heard the sirens shortly after closing and locking his front door. He had known exactly where they were going. Sleep had finally come to him just past 4:00 in the morning. He had woken at half past noon and spent the next half hour waiting for a knock on his door. When none came he had finally started to relax. He sat on the couch, his sock covered feet on the coffee table, and looked through the file he had stolen from the lawyer's office. He had already gone through it once and found nothing related to his grandfather, but figured a second time before he destroyed it couldn't hurt. As he paged through it again he thought about everything that had occurred during his time in Taos. The death of the old man, his grandfather's rapidly declining health, hitting the lawyer in the head, and burning the contents of the storage unit made quite a list. He found himself thinking about the old man's house again. He had searched it thoroughly yet had the niggling feeling in the back of his mind that he had somehow missed something.

. . .

Tony decided that rather than sitting around obsessing over it, he would simply go back to the house and have another look around. He wasn't sure what he would do if the old man's son was there. Tony didn't bother himself with that. He had been lucky thus far and his luck was sure to hold out one more time. Just as he was walking out his front door the thought occurred to him. Rather than searching the house, he would simply burn it down. He dumped three more beers down the sink and filled the bottles with gas in the same way he had the previous evening. He was dressed in dark jeans, a sweatshirt, boots, and his heavy jacket. The day was clear and bright, but the wind was frigid. He put the Molotov cocktails and the gas can in his truck and headed out.

There were no cars in the driveway of the old man's house, which Tony took to be a good sign. He parked in the driveway, slid out of the truck, and approached the front door. He knocked loudly and received no response. A turn of the door handle revealed that it was locked so he started making his way around the house looking for a window to break. He came across another door on the side of the house and tried it. It opened. Tony couldn't help but smile as he stepped into the house. He walked through it quickly making sure that it was indeed empty. It looked much the same as it had when he had last been inside, the exception a stack of paintings leaning against the living room wall and a box of clay figurines near the living room fireplace.

. . .

Tony returned to his truck and brought the gas filled beer bottles and the gas can into the house. He had briefly considered keeping a few of the paintings. They were all obviously valuable. Keeping something that could tie him to the old man seemed a reckless idea however, and in the end he decided to use them as kindling. As he was crossing the living room his boot caught on the edge of the rug and he nearly fell down. His arms reflexively reached out to his sides to steady himself and the lighter he carried loosely in his left hand flew out of his grip and slid across the floor. It landed just underneath the record player cabinet. Tony kicked at the rug in anger, then took a calming breath and knelt down next to the cabinet. When he looked underneath his eyes widened in surprise and a slow smile spread across his face. Lying right next to the lighter was a handgun.

100

LOYAL TRUESDALE

Loyal set his phone on the table and considered what the detective had just told him. He thought about the odds that the intruder would return to his father's house and considered it unlikely. The man had been unconscious and bleeding from the head when he was driven away in the ambulance. Loyal was confidant he had needed stitches and had been concussed. The most logical assumption was that he had returned to wherever he had come from to lick his wounds and rest. He thought back to his movements before he had left the house. He clearly remembered locking the front door but was unsure now if he had locked the door to the mud room.

Loyal stuffed the last of his tacos in his mouth and stood. He removed two twenties from his wallet and threw them on the table then walked quickly through the restaurant and to the Tahoe. He slid in and drove towards his father's house. He felt a sense of urgency he could not explain. He reached down and felt the outline of the PM9 on his waist. If the intruder was back he was going down. And this time he would not be getting up again.

101

ANTONIO SHAW

Tony lay flat on the floor and reached under the cabinet. He brought the lighter out first then very gingerly slid the gun toward him. When it was clear of the cabinet he sat up and lifted it to examine it. It was a beautiful gun. The word Kimber was embedded into what Tony thought looked like brown alligator trim on the grip. He slipped off his gloves to get a better feel for the gun. He wasn't concerned about fingerprints, he was keeping this for himself. Tony stood up and inspected the gun. Holding it in his right hand he used his left to push up the slide stop and lock the slide to the rear. This action ejected the round that was in the chamber. He caught it in his hand. He released the magazine and reinstalled the round. He reinserted the magazine and released the slide. After securing the hammer he tucked the gun in his waistband and turned back to his task at hand.

He splashed gas on the paintings, around the bedroom, and across the living room floor. He unlocked the front door and opened it. His plan was to go outside and then throw the molotov cocktails through the front door. With the amount of gasoline he had spread throughout the house he knew it was going to ignite instantly. Just as he was stepping onto the front porch he heard the sound of a vehicle coming down the drive. He quickly stepped back into the house and partially closed the front door. He watched through the narrow rectangular window beside the front door as a Chevy Tahoe approached and parked horizontally behind his truck, effectively blocking him in. He watched as the old man's son slid out of the vehicle and slipped behind the shed.

102

WALKER TRUESDALE - MARCH 2, 1972

Barrossa did not contact Walker for over a month. Walker was beginning to relax and to allow himself to believe that the whole mess was behind him. He had said nothing to Rita about any of it and was glad now that he hadn't. The good feeling vanished on a Thursday as he left work. From a distance he saw that someone was leaning against his truck in the parking lot. Although he couldn't see the person's features from such a distance, Walker instinctively knew exactly who it was. He approached his truck cautiously keeping an eye out for the two men who always seemed to travel with Barrossa. As he got closer he saw them. Two figures dressed in dark suits and maintaining a respectful distance from their boss.

Barrossa spoke first. "You have my money?" he asked.

"I told you it is not my debt to pay," said Walker.

Barrossa smiled but the smile did not reach his eyes.

"Family debt is family debt," he said. "You can't just walk away from it."

"What are you going to do," asked Walker, "kill me too? Then there's no one left to pay.

Barrossa didn't smile as he said, "There's always someone to pay."

A chill settled over Walker as he thought about his wife and son. He wondered if Barrossa would be so cruel as to harm Rita or Loyal.

"Leave my family out of this Barrossa," he said through clenched teeth.

Barrossa smiled that cold smile again. "Your two months are up on the twenty-first of this month. But you know what Walker, I'm a generous man." He pushed off Walker's truck and started to walk away, then turned back.

"I'll give you a couple of extra weeks. Two weeks from this Friday. Not a day more."

Walker watched Barrossa slide into the backseat of a forest green Cadillac Fleetwood Eldorado. One of his men slid into the driver's seat, the other joined Barrossa in the backseat. None of them glanced at Walker as they drove away.

Walker stood still for a few minutes and replayed the conversation with Barrossa in his mind. How could he best protect Rita and Loyal? Finally he turned away from his truck and walked back into General Dynamics. He went directly to the Human Resources office and tendered his resignation, effective immediately. He returned to his truck and drove home. That night, as they lay in bed, Walker tried to think of a way to share his predicament with Rita but found he simply could not find the words. In the end he decided the less she knew the better it would be for her. The only way he could protect his family was to leave them.

103

LOYAL TRUESDALE

Loyal saw the truck parked in his driveway as soon as he turned off the main road. He felt it unlikely that the morning's intruder would be so bold as to park in front of the house. Still, he wasn't going to take any chances so he parked the Tahoe sideways to block the truck in as much as possible. He slid out of the Tahoe, PM9 in his right hand and held by his side, and walked quickly behind the shed. He stood by the back corner and peered at his father's house. He saw no one and sensed no movement, yet something was off. It took him about thirty seconds to realize what that was. The scent of gasoline was wafting in the air. An image of the burned storage unit flashed through Loyal's mind.

Just as he stepped away from the shed toward the house a shot rang out. Loyal heard the bullet hit the shed as he ducked back behind it. Two more shots followed the first in quick succession. Loyal heard one whiz by his left side and another hit the shed with a loud thump. A wave of anger surged through Loyal.

He sprinted away from the shed toward the house firing several shots to provide some type of cover. He skidded to a stop on the front porch just to the left of the partially opened front door and the narrow rectangular window beside it. Loyal risked a peek through the narrow window. A man dressed in black stood in the living room. His profile was visible to Loyal, but his face was not Loyal's concern. The man held what was clearly a homemade Molotov cocktail in his left hand. In his right hand he held a lighter. With no hesitation Loyal stepped into the house and fired the PM9. The bullet hit the man in the upper back at exactly the same time as he ignited the improvised wick. The force of the impact caused his arms to splay out to his sides. Loyal watched in seemingly slow motion as the bottle flew from the man's left hand and crashed into the fireplace. The bottle shattered and immediately burst into flames.

Loyal ran through the house to where the man lay. He hooked his wrists beneath each of the man's arms and, PM9 still in his right hand, dragged him toward the mud room door. The flames were growing rapidly, feeding hungrily on the gasoline and paintings. The extreme heat burned Loyal's skin and lungs as he pulled the motionless man from the house. When he was far enough away from the house that he no longer felt the scorching heat from the nearly fully engulfed structure. he lowered the man, facedown, to the ground. Loyal frisked him and found the Kimber in his waistband. He removed it and placed it in his own coat pocket. He slid his phone out of his pants pocket and, for the second time that day, dialed 911.

104

ANTONIO SHAW

Tony was conscious but weak. He had been surprised when the old man's son had rushed through the flames and pulled him out of the house. When the bullet had hit him and knocked him to the floor his first thought had been that he was going to die in the fire. He felt the Kimber being removed from his waistband and listened as Loyal called 911. The left side of Tony's face was in the snow. He tried to turn himself and realized that he did not have the strength. He found himself wondering if, perhaps, his unbelievable luck had finally run out.

105

LOYAL TRUESDALE

Loyal ended the 911 call and turned his attention back to the arsonist. He removed a glove from his coat pocket and pressed it against the wound on the man's left shoulder, then rolled him over so that he could see his face. His eyes were open but his face was slack and his skin was pale. Loyal glanced at his father's house. It was completely engulfed in flames. Loyal knew that nothing could be salvaged. It was a total loss. He looked back at the man on the ground. His eyes were closed now, his breathing shallow. Loyal's first instinct was to punch the guy, but he knew there was no point now. As he looked at the man's face a gradual sense of recognition began to form in Loyal's mind. He knew this man somehow. Loyal remained on his knees beside the man and gazed at his face. The name, when it finally popped into his mind, hit Loyal with force.

Three things had happened in Loyal's life to end his motorcycle racing "career". The trio of events were becoming an officer, getting married, and becoming a father. There was simply no time for racing, especially after Michelle left and he became a single father. Once a year, however, he participated in the annual Fire & Police Motocross Nationals. Loyal had raced in the first race which was held at Perris Raceway in November of 1989. He had continued to race each year until his mid forties. He always made sure to invite Marco Barrossa to come out and watch. Barrossa showed up each year and always brought his young grandson Tony along. Looking at the face of the arsonist now, Loyal was absolutely sure this was Tony.

He rocked back on his heels as memories of time spent with Barrossa flooded his brain. They had traveled together to Baja and raced locally at Carlsbad, Perris, and Saddleback. Loyal had never completely understood why Barrossa sponsored him, but he had never questioned it. There was no way his mother could have afforded the bikes, gear, travel, and entry fees. The one thing that had always annoyed Loyal, though he would never say anything and risk Barrossa pulling his support, was that the man was always bringing up Loyal's father in casual conversation. He'd say things like, "Heard from your old man?" or "Bet you wish your Dad was here." In much the same way as lock pins align in a tumbler lock, Loyal's thoughts and memories lined up in such a way that he saw things with a clarity he had lacked his entire life. Marco Barrossa had been looking for his father.

The first responders arrived, as did the detective who had been at the house earlier in the day. The time passed in a haze for Loyal. He watched as Tony was loaded into the ambulance and driven away. He recited the afternoon's events for the detective and was disappointed to hear the man, his name was Detective Mendoza, say that this interview would have to be completed at the station. The detective allowed Loyal to drive his own car and follow him to the station which, like nearly every other place Loyal had been during the week, was located in Historic Taos. They found parking in the lot and entered through a back door. Detective Mendoza set Loyal up in interview room 2, stepped out briefly, then returned with two cups of coffee. He handed one to Loyal as he sat down.

"This interview is being recorded," he said. Loyal nodded but remained silent. "I'm the only detective in this department," he said, "and I've been busy as hell these past two days. Three incidents lead me back to you." He held up his right pointer finger. "Arson at Hinds and Hinds," he added his middle finger to the pointer, "the attack at your place this morning," his ring finger joined the other two, "and now a shooting at your place this afternoon." He lowered his hands and leaned forward, elbows on the table that separated the two men. His eyes found Loyal's. "What the hell is going on?"

Loyal took his time and walked the detective through then entire sequence of events one more time. He began with Francine Blackwater's call the previous Monday and ended with the shooting at his father's house. The only bit he left out was recognizing Tony. He told the detective he had no idea who the man who had burned his father's house down was. Detective Mendoza was well aware that Francine had been attacked in her office and added her case to the three he had listed for

Loyal already. He questioned Loyal for well over an hour. At the end of the interview Loyal asked if there had been any news regarding the man who had attacked O'Keefe. Mendoza shook his head.

"We are working on the assumption that he stole the nurse's phone and called an Uber. We have been to the house where he was apparently dropped off but it is empty. It is owned by a corporation. I'm working on a search warrant now. We also have pictures of him taken at the hospital, but no ID. I had an officer show the pictures to businesses around town, but she hasn't come up with anything yet." He paused for a moment, then said, "Your gun is going to have to stay here until this whole thing is settled. I don't see the D.A. calling this anything but self defense. Still, we need it until the case is closed."

106

LOYAL TRUESDALE

Loyal slid into Trinity's rental and closed the door. He started the engine and then realized he had nowhere to go. He slid his phone out and googled places to stay in Taos. The Hotel la Fonda de Taos looked as good as any others and was close. He drove there and booked a deluxe king room through Sunday. The deluxe was actually two rooms; a bedroom with a king sized bed and a sitting room with a couch, table, and television. Loyal sat heavily on the couch and considered his situation. He had nothing but the clothes on his back, his empty belly band, his phone, his wallet, and two sets of keys; his father's set and Trinity's rental key. As he sat there the enormity of what he had lost enveloped him. Everything his father had left him was destroyed. The familiar anger at his father from his youth surged through Loyal's veins again. If Walker hadn't left everything he owned to Loyal none of this would have happened. Francine would likely still be fine, the storage unit and the house wouldn't have been burned, and, Trinity, by far the most important factor, wouldn't have said they needed to take a break.

. . .

Loyal looked at the pictures he had taken of the burned out storage unit and his father's house in flames. He tapped the message icon, chose a few pictures from each scene, and sent them to Trinity. The only words he included in the message were *It's all gone.* He waited five minutes to see if she would respond. She did not. Loyal stood with a sigh. It looked like Trinity had meant what she had said.

107

TRINITY GLASS

Trinity was just finishing dinner in her hotel room when her phone pinged. When she saw the sender of the text she simply shook her head. Her first instinct was to set the phone down and ignore Loyal's message, but her curiosity got the best of her and she opened it up. She read the words *it's all gone* then scrolled through the pictures he had included. Her shoulders slumped as she looked at the destruction. Something Loyal had said right before she left Taos came into her mind. He had said he felt like throwing a match on everything. She wondered if he might actually have done just that. She considered the possibility then rejected it. Loyal wasn't destructive and he certainly wouldn't have done that kind of damage to the storage unit. More likely he would have just hauled everything out to the dump.

With a small gasp of pain, Trinity rose from the table and lay down on the bed. She was both mentally and physically exhausted. As promised, she had shown up for work at noon.

Caldwell had offered for her to go back to the hotel to rest and return on Monday, but she had refused. The day had been long and the tension between Trinity and Caldwell thick. The relief she had felt when five o'clock rolled around had been tremendous, yet the weekend loomed in front of her like a never ending tunnel.

Trinity lay on the bed and mentally reviewed all the things that had been lost to fire in Taos. She raised her right hand and looked at the turquoise ring on her finger. This was, perhaps, the only thing left out of all Walker's belongings. She thought about the paintings and clay figurines they had so painstakingly researched. Valuable art, most of the artists long dead, turned into ash. Her heart ached for Loyal. The mystery of his father's disappearance would remain. The answers he had long hoped for would never be revealed. She closed her eyes then opened them again. Something still did remain. She worked her way into a sitting position then stood. She walked to the bathroom and picked up the plastic bag from the hospital that contained the clothes she had been wearing when she was pushed off the road. She had almost thrown them away this morning and was grateful now that she had not. She pulled her jacket from the bag, reached into the pocket, and grabbed the items she had stuffed into it at the storage unit. She removed her hand from the pocket and opened it. The stack of twenties had survived.

108

WALKER TRUESDALE - APRIL 7, 1971

Loyal's eleventh birthday was both one of the best and one of the worst days of Walker's life. He had picked his son up early from school. When they got home and went inside a new Yamaha motorcycle had been parked in front of the fireplace. Walker and Loyal had spent the better part of the afternoon riding around the property. Rita had made Loyal's favorite dinner and a chocolate cake for dessert. Walker, aware this was his last night with his beloved family, had watched with a heavy heart as Loyal made a wish and blew out the candles. He had hoped Loyal had made a good one and that it would somehow come true. After Loyal had gone to bed, Walker had put the John Prine album on the record player and danced with Rita. The thought of even one day without her by his side or one night without her in his arms had been more than he could bear. In his wildest dreams he never could have imagined a day when he would leave her. He had tightened his arms around his wife and, since her head was on his chest and she could not see his face, he had let the teardrops fall.

. . .

At 2:00 am Walker, dressed in faded jeans and a ratty old sweatshirt and holding a backpack in his hands, stood at the door to his son's room. He set the backpack by his feet and leaned against the doorway. Loyal was sleeping deeply. Walker watched his son's chest rise and fall with his rhythmic breathing. A tear pricked at Walker's eye, but he blinked it back. This was not the time for sentimentality. Walker's own decisions, all bad he realized now, had led to this moment. His wife and son could never know the reason for his abandoning them. They would wake in the morning and simply find him gone. As the hours passed, and he did not return, they would become worried. Rita would notify the Sheriff, but nothing would come of the search. He would never be found. Walker tried to tell himself that he was doing this for his family, to protect them. In some ways this was true. The more accurate reason, however, was self protection.

Walker watched his son and thought about Loyal's birthday celebration. He pictured the expression on Loyal's face when he had presented him with the brand new motorcycle and his eyes filled again. A tear escaped Walker's eye this time and slipped slowly down his cheek. Loyal was a good kid. While Walker would never see him grow into a man, he was sure that Loyal would be a good one. Better than Walker was. Walker wiped his cheek with the back of his hand, picked up the backpack and walked away.

109

LOYAL TRUESDALE

The lack of a response from Trinity reminded Loyal again that she wanted a break from him. The rumbling from his stomach reminded him that he had eaten little this day. He googled places to eat near Hotel la Fonda and settled on The Gorge Bar and Grill which google informed him was a simple two minute walk from his hotel. Precipitation was once again coming from the sky, this time in the form of sleet. Loyal pulled the hood of his jacket over his head and walked quickly through the falling pellets. The sun had gone down hours previously. The black night was illuminated by the old fashioned street lamps along the sidewalk.

The bar was crowded despite the weather. Loyal was seated at a table for two. He ordered a margarita on the rocks to sip while he studied the menu. The tables were set fairly close together so he was able to see and smell the food being delivered to other patrons. Everything looked delicious. In the end he decided on a Gorge cut ribeye that came with blue cheese mashed potatoes and vegetables. He ordered another margarita when he placed his dinner order. By the time his food was served he was ready for another drink. Loyal was well on his way to getting drunk. He was aware of this and he did not care. In fact he welcomed it. The entire Taos experience had been a shit show from beginning to end. Oblivion would be welcomed.

When he left The Gorge Loyal had consumed five margaritas. The dinner had been excellent and he was finally feeling no mental pain. He walked through the sleet, this time without his hood covering his head, and let the cold pellets sting his face. His hair became saturated in the few minutes it took him to walk to his hotel room. He realized he was wearing his father's coat, not his own. It kept him warm. He entered and went straight to the bathroom where he stripped off his wet clothes and stepped into a steaming shower. Fifteen minutes later he was wrapped in a bathrobe provided by the hotel and sitting on the couch. He checked his phone and saw a missed call from Stella. She had not left a voicemail. He tried to think back to the last time he had communicated with her. He was able to remember, in spite of his tequila infused brain, that it had been several days. He wasn't sure if he was up to talking to her and wondered if she would be able to tell that he was drunk over the phone.

"What the hell," he said out loud and he tapped her name.

Loyal told Stella about everything except the break from Trinity and his recognition of Tony. Stella and Tony had actually played together at the annual Fire/Police motocross races and Loyal had taken Stella with him on some of his occasional visits to Barrossa at his home in Rancho Santa Fe. If she recognized that he was drunk by the sound of his voice Stella kept it to herself. She was dismayed to hear of all the destruction of her grandfather's things and relieved that Loyal had not sustained any injuries.

"When are you coming home Dad?" she asked. "Boo misses you." She paused a moment then added, "We all do."

"Probably a day or two," said Loyal. "I want to go look at the remains of the house tomorrow. I don't think anything survived, but I feel like I should check. I miss you guys too."

110

LOYAL TRUESDALE

Loyal dreamed of fire. Red, yellow, and orange flames danced in front of his eyes. Images of people flickered in his vision as well; his father and mother, Stella, Trinity, O'Keefe, Francine, Barrossa, and Tony. He tried to reach out and touch the images of those he cared about but they would twitch and jerk away from his hand as if in spasm. When he woke in the predawn hours Loyal found himself twisted in his blankets and sweating profusely. He disentangled himself clumsily and slid out of bed. He made a very necessary trip to the bathroom then returned to the bed and lay down again. The good feeling he had enjoyed the night before from the tequila was gone. It had been replaced by a raging headache.

Loyal drifted in and out of sleep for several hours. Eventually he rose and pulled back the blackout curtains so he could look out the window. The early morning light was gray and sleet was still falling. Loyal let the curtain drop back into place and went in search of the coffee machine. He took another shower while the coffee brewed, then sat on the couch in the hotel robe and tried to formulate some type of a plan for the day. He found himself repeatedly checking his phone for a response from Trinity. In his head he knew that if she was going to respond she would have done so by now. His heart was a different story. He realized if he was going to get anything done this day he would have to stop thinking about her. He mentally boxed up his feelings for Trinity and stored them away in a corner of his mind. He would open the mental box sometime in the future when he had the time and the inclination to explore the contents. With thoughts of Trinity stashed away his brain was free to make plans for the day.

When his mental list was complete Loyal dressed in the only clothes he had; yesterday's. The sleet was still falling as he drove to a clothing store called Re-Threads. He bought clothes and a duffel bag and changed in the dressing room. He then drove to Albertson's and purchased toiletries. Once he had everything he needed he did a google search on breakfast in Taos. A restaurant called Michael's Kitchen looked good and was less than ten minutes away. He passed Hinds and Hinds on his way and decided to stop in after breakfast and talk to Dave about the cleanup of his storage unit. He assumed he would be financially responsible and wanted to make arrangements as soon as possible. Michael's Kitchen was a restaurant and a bakery. Loyal loaded up on huevos rancheros and coffee then bought two apple fritters for later. Before he drove to Hinds and Hinds he called Francine's doctor to check on her status. The call went to voicemail. Loyal left a brief message asking the doctor to call when it was convenient.

. . .

Dave was at his desk when Loyal entered the office of Hinds and Hinds.

"Hey there Mr. Truesdale," he said indicating a chair with a wave of his hand, "have a seat."

Loyal removed his coat and hung it on a rack in the corner of the office. He sat in the chair opposite Dave and leaned forward.

"I'm assuming I have some responsibility for the clean up of the unit," he said. "I'd like to arrange that now if we could."

Dave folded his hands on the desk.

"It needs to be cleaned out once the scene is released by fire, police, and the insurance company but I believe the insurance company will cover the cleaning," he said.

"You have my phone and credit card number. Will you call if there are any additional charges for me?" asked Loyal. "I'm leaving Taos soon."

"That works," said Dave. Loyal reached across the desk and shook Dave's hand. "Thanks for everything Dave."

111

LOYAL TRUESDALE

The last stop on Loyal's mental list was going to be the most difficult. He drove down the drive to his father's house with apprehension. The sleet was falling harder now making visibility poor. Still, he was able to make out the pile of rubble that had, just yesterday, been a beautiful home. He parked by the shed and slid out of the Tahoe. He pulled the zipper of his coat up to his chin and slid the hood over his head. He removed his one remaining glove from his pocket and slipped it on his left hand, then turned toward what was left of the house. Both chimneys were still standing and easy to distinguish from the mess. Everything else was ash and rubble on the ground.

Loyal stepped gingerly through the rubble. He pictured the layout of the house in his mind. Before leaving his hotel room he had googled *what does not melt in a house fire* and had learned that a typical house burns at 1,100 degrees Fahrenheit. Jewelry was listed as an item that can withstand that type of heat. Loyal was hoping to find his father's wedding ring and the necklace he had kept for Stella. He knew it was a long shot but still he wanted to try.

He started in the area that had been his father's bedroom. The ring had been in the drawer of the end table next to the bed. He knelt down and began sifting through the remains of his father's life. The sleet was still falling steadily and the skin on his ungloved hand was stinging from the cold. Still, he persisted, and was pleased when his nearly numb fingers found the ring. Despite his anger he still wanted to have some memento to remind him of his father. He slipped the ring into his pants pocket, blew warm breath on his hand and slid it into the coat pocket to warm for a moment. He walked to the area where he thought Stella's necklace might have been and began sifting through rubble again. He used his gloved left hand and kept his right in his pocket. He spent about twenty minutes searching but found nothing.

Loyal stood and walked to the living room fireplace. He ran his left hand over the rocks. The memory of him sitting in the chair with Trinity in his lap floated into his mind. He pushed it away. He turned in a slow circle, taking in the destruction, and wondering what he was going to do with this property now. As he turned something caught his eye. A scratched beige corner of something was poking up in the area that had been the mud room. Loyal walked to it and knelt down. He used his gloved hand to push the debris away from the object eventually revealing what looked like an old safe. Loyal rocked back on his heels and studied it. He and Trinity had searched the entire house and never seen this. Loyal supposed it could have been hidden beneath the floorboards. He estimated it's size to be about 15" by 20". It was definitely old and had a thin handle and a covered keyhole. Loyal tried to move it and was surprised by its weight. He pulled his father's keys out of his pocket intending to try the small mystery key in the lock but then thought better of that. The sleet could easily damage whatever might be inside.

Loyal walked back to the shed. There were holes on the side of it where the bullets had been removed by the crime scene techs. He opened the door and found the tarp that had been covering the snowplow just to the left of the door exactly where he had placed it. He carried the tarp back to the safe, opened it, and pulled it over himself and the safe. Now that the safe was protected from the sleet he tried the key. It slid in easily and turned. With butterflies in his stomach, Loyal pulled the handle and opened the safe. The door was heavy and nearly three inches thick. Once he had it open Loyal looked inside.

The first thing he saw was a gun. He reached in and picked it up with his ungloved hand. He recognized it immediately as a Colt 357 Python. Loyal opened the cylinder. The gun was unloaded. He closed the cylinder and slipped the Python into his belly band. Although it was unloaded Loyal still felt better just to be carrying a gun. He'd buy ammunition before he left New Mexico. The next thing he lifted out of the safe was a photograph. Loyal recognized all three men in the picture.

Marco Barrossa was in the middle. His Uncle Jamison was on one side and his father was on the other. The last thing in the safe was a well worn brown leather journal. Loyal lifted it slowly feeling the weight of it in his hands. A smile spread slowly across his face. Turns out his father had left him a birthday box after all.

112

ANTONIO SHAW

Tony remembered little of what had transpired after he was brought by ambulance to the hospital. He had been rushed into surgery and then slept through the night in a haze of pain medication. The doctor had backed off the pain medication a bit on Saturday and Tony was no longer able to drift in and out. The pain in his left shoulder was severe. His right wrist was handcuffed to the bed railing making it impossible for Tony to shift his body in an attempt to alleviate the pain. He had been placed under arrest and allowed a phone call. He had called his grandfather's lawyer, Amos Wentworth, who had assured him that he was on his way to Taos. Tony had seen Wentworth work his magic before and was feeling confidant that he would serve little time. Detective Mendoza had tried to get some type of statement out of Tony but he had refused to say anything without legal representation.

The wound to his shoulder was a problem. The bullet had impacted the brachial plexus which is a network of nerves that sends signals from the spine to the shoulder, arm, and hand. The doctor had informed him that he would need at least two more surgeries and would likely suffer from pain and some loss of motor function for the rest of his life. Tony knew that he was lucky to be alive. The old man's son had risked his own life to drag Tony out of the inferno he had created. He brought the image of the fully engulfed home into his mind and couldn't help but smile despite the pain in his shoulder. He had accomplished what he had set out to do. Everything connected to the old man had been destroyed. No connection between the old man and his grandfather could possibly remain.

113

LOYAL TRUESDALE

Loyal slipped the photograph inside the journal and then tucked the journal into the inside pocket of his coat. He closed and relocked the safe, then stood and let the tarp fall to the ground. He walked back to the Tahoe and slid in. He considered opening the journal immediately, but decided against it. Instead he pulled the journal out of his pocket, picked up the picture Trinity had set in the cupholder, slid it into the journal, and returned the journal to his pocket. He had finally found the key to his father's desertion and he wanted to do this right. He drove first to a local gun store, Gunslingers, and purchased ammunition for his father's Python, a locking gun case, and an ammo box. He loaded the gun in the Tahoe and slid it back into his belly band. Feeling fully dressed again, he drove to Albertson's and bought a bottle of Jack Daniels whiskey, the same brand he had seen in his father's house. His errands done, he drove back to the Hotel la Fonda de Taos and parked. The sleet had stopped. The air was very cold and the sky was a clear bright blue. On impulse he walked to the Gorge Bar and Grill and ordered two hamburgers to go. He carried all his supplies into his hotel room and locked the door. He set the whiskey and the burgers on the coffee table then carefully removed the journal from his inside jacket pocket. He held it for a long moment then placed it next to the whiskey. He removed his belly band and lay that on the table too. His plan was to shower, raise a toast to his father, then read.

He had taken a few steps toward the bathroom when his phone rang. The only call he was expecting was from Francine's doctor. The only call he was hoping for was from Trinity. He looked at the caller ID and saw it was neither of those people, the caller was Maynard Lily.

"Maynard," he said, "how are you?"

"I'm doing better thanks to you," said Maynard. "The local FBI agents are paying a lot closer attention to my case since your friend got involved. Can you thank her for me?"

"Sure," said Loyal. "Any news about your money?"

"Not yet," said Maynard, "but I'm hopeful. For now I'm selling the Rancho Santa Fe house and all but one of our rental houses. Keeping one in Carlsbad for us to live in."

"I'm sorry about that man," said Loyal. "I know how much you all love that house."

"It was too big for the three of us anyways," said Maynard. "You still in Taos?"

In much the same way he had with Detective Mendoza, Loyal spent the next ten minutes filling Maynard in on everything that had happened since he had arrived in Taos. He left out any mention of the safe and its contents. Maynard offered to deal with the rental agency regarding the totaled truck and Loyal gratefully accepted his offer. They agreed to meet for lunch once Loyal was back in California and said goodbye. Loyal showered and dressed in the hotel robe once more. He sat on the couch and poured a small amount of whiskey into a glass. He held the glass out in front of him and conjured up a mental image of his father.

"Here's to you Dad," he said, "and the secrets you are about to reveal." He drank the shot of whiskey and set the glass on the table. He picked up the journal, opened it to the first page, and began to read.

114

LOYAL TRUESDALE

Loyal left Taos at noon on Sunday. Francine's doctor returned his call as he was checking out of Hotel La Fonda. He explained that although Francine was still in a coma, the swelling in her brain was lessening and the bone flap was scheduled to be replaced later in the day. He stressed that she was far from being out of the woods yet. His final words to Loyal had been, "I'm cautiously optimistic."

Loyal had stayed up most of the night, slept a few hours, then gotten up again to finish reading his father's journal. The simmering anger that had always surrounded thoughts of his father was now boiling and directed completely at Marco Barrossa. Walker had recorded the whole story of his life with Rita and Loyal, the issues with Jameson and his murder, and the debt being transferred to him. The only thing he had left out was the manner in which he had acquired the money for Jameson. The last part of the journal was full of his deep regret that he had left his family. He had loved them until his last day on earth. The last entry before Walker's "suicide" had sent chills down Loyal's spine.

I felt eyes on me again today. It is the third day in a row that I have felt this sensation. He's out there. I can feel it. And it is ok. I'm tired and ready to be with Rita again.

He thought about these words again as he drove out of town. The day was cold and clear, the first day without snow or sleet since Loyal had arrived in Taos. The sun shone brightly in the sky but provided no warmth. The view of the Rio Grande was spectacular. The road took him along the upper course of the Rio Grande. The river was full and roaring, the water rolling and tumbling. Whitecaps were created by the force of the water. Loyal found a spot to pull over. He slid out of the Tahoe and stood looking down at the water. He ignored the frigid air that buffeted his body and blew through his hair. Images flicked through his mind like a slide show; Walker, Rita, Trinity. He thought about all he had lost and what he had gained. For a fraction of a second the impulse to simply step off the edge and plummet to the roaring water slipped into his brain. He shook it off, slid back in the Tahoe and continued his drive.

Loyal stopped at Maria's in Santa Fe for a late lunch. His flight out of Albuquerque was scheduled to leave at 6:00 pm so he had plenty of time. He ordered a margarita this time. The drinks menu was extensive. He finally decided on a Turquoise Trail which was made with Sauza Blue 100% agave Reposado tequila and Blue Curacao. He ordered Maria's combination plate which consisted of one enchilada, one taco, one tamale, one Chile relleno, rice, and beans. It was a lot of food and he ate slowly, savoring the tastes. He knew the drive from Santa Fe would take just over one hour and he was in no rush. As long as he dropped Trinity's rental off by 4:30 he would have plenty of time to take the tram to the airport and to check his bag. His hand moved to the belly band on his waist and he smiled.

115

LOYAL TRUESDALE

Loyal pulled up to the car rental office at 4:35 fully expecting to have to pay for the extra days he had been driving the Tahoe. Trinity had always planned to leave by Friday, so he assumed he would have to pay for Saturday and Sunday and probably some fees for having kept the vehicle longer than he was supposed to. He was surprised to find that Trinity had extended the rental agreement through Monday so he was actually dropping the Tahoe off early. Although he knew he would not get a response he texted her a quick thank you while he was riding the tram to the airport.

Because of the time difference between New Mexico and California, Loyal landed at Ontario at 6:34, seemingly only thirty four minutes after he had taken off. He collected his duffel at baggage claim and walked out to his truck. The sun had set several hours previously and the parking lot was dark and quiet. He texted Stella from his truck and told her he would be home in a few hours then started up the truck and headed for the freeway.

Loyal drove through In and Out on the way home and picked up a double double for himself and a plain patty for Boo. He parked in the driveway and carried the food and his belongings into the house. His father's gun was in the belly band on his waist and the journal was tucked safely inside his jacket's inner pocket. The house was silent when he entered. A single living room light had been left on for him. He could see Boo on the cat post, curled in a ball and fast asleep. Loyal set his duffel bag on the floor next to the couch and the bag of food on the coffee table. He got a beer from the fridge, opened it, and took a long pull. Boo looked up at the sound of the bottle opening. When he saw Loyal he gave himself a long leisurely stretch then hopped off the cat post and trotted over to the couch. Loyal set the beer on the coffee table and picked up the little cat. He petted him for a moment then sat on the couch and opened the bag from In and Out. He broke Boo's patty into pieces and the little guy sat on the coffee table to eat. When both of them had finished their food Boo hopped into Loyal's lap, curled up, and went back to sleep.

Loyal leaned back against the couch cushions and let out a long sigh. He took another pull off the beer and closed his eyes. He was just drifting off when he heard Stella say, "Hey Dad." He opened his eyes and looked up at her.

"Hey," he said.

She sat on the couch beside him. He wrapped his left arm around her, and pulled her close.

"Sorry we didn't wait up for you," she said, "we sleep when Mason does."

Loyal smiled. "I remember those days," he said. He reached into his jacket with his right hand and removed the journal.

"Is that grandpa's journal?" Stella asked.

Loyal nodded.

"You want to talk about it?" asked Stella.

Loyal shook his head and handed the journal to Stella. "You should read this first," he said.

Loyal removed his arm from Stella's shoulder and set Boo gently on the couch. He stood and gathered the remains of their dinner. He tossed the wrappers in the trash, drained his beer, then added the bottle to the trash can.

"I'm going to bed," he said as he gathered Boo from the couch.

"I love you Dad," said Stella.

"I love you too kiddo," said Loyal. He opened his bedroom door, stepped inside, and shut it quietly behind him.

116

LOYAL TRUESDALE

Loyal woke to an insistent pinching on his left hand. He opened his eyes and saw Boo gently biting his fingers.

"You need to go to the bathroom buddy?" Loyal said quietly. He slid out of bed and opened the bedroom door for the cat, then pulled on his robe and stepped out into the living room. He walked to the kitchen to start a pot of coffee and was surprised to see that the time was 10:13. He had slept for over twelve hours. When he turned to get a mug out of the cabinet he saw his father's journal sitting on the kitchen counter. A folded piece of paper sat on top of the journal. He opened it and saw it was a note from Stella.

Hey, Dad,

We are heading home. Sorry not to say goodbye, but I didn't want to wake you. I'm sure you needed the sleep. I read the entire journal last night. Call me when you are ready to talk.

. . .

Loyal definitely wanted to talk to Stella, but she was not the first person on his list. That space belonged to Marco Barrossa. After feeding Boo and drinking two cups of very strong coffee, Loyal dressed in faded jeans and a flannel. The shirt hung loosely over his belly band and the Python. He hadn't made a solid plan regarding his visit to Marco Barrossa. His initial anger at the man had morphed into something darker and deeper. A feeling unlike any he had ever experienced. It sat in the pit of his belly like a molten rock radiating heat and fury. If his father's journal was accurate, and Loyal had no reason to believe that it was not, then Marco Barrossa was singlehandedly responsible for the destruction of Loyal's family. The man had to pay.

A light rain began to fall as Loyal slid into his truck and backed out of the driveway. He drove south on the Coast Highway rather than taking the freeway. The ocean and sky were identical shades of gray. When looking out towards the horizon it was impossible to tell where one ended and the other began. Traffic was light and Loyal drove at a leisurely pace. He turned left at Lomas Santa Fe and drove up the hill into Rancho Santa Fe. He pulled up to Marco Barrossa's gate and waited for the guard to come out of the guardhouse. The guard approached the truck, umbrella over his head, and looked at Loyal inquiringly.

"Loyal Truesdale for Marco Barrossa," said Loyal.

"He's not taking visitors," said the guard.

"Tell him it is Loyal Truesdale and that I've just returned from New Mexico," said Loyal, "I'm confidant he'll see me."

The guard returned to the guardhouse. Loyal could see through the window that he was on the phone. After several minutes the gate opened. Loyal drove through and parked near the front door of the house. He slid out of the truck and walked quickly through the rain to the front door.

A middle aged woman answered the door. Her brown hair was pulled back in a severe pony tail. She was dressed in dark blue scrubs and wore round tortoiseshell glasses. Her expression was not a happy one. "I've advised him against seeing you," she said, "but he insists. You can have five minutes."

Loyal nodded but said nothing. He followed the nurse through the giant living room. Loyal saw everything in a different light now. Marco Barrossa's wealth used to impress him, now it just made him sick. The nurse opened a heavy wooden door and walked through it. Loyal followed. The room was dimly lit and it took a moment for Loyal's eyes to adjust. When he brought Marco Barrossa into focus he was shocked. The man was dwarfed by the giant king sized bed in which he lay. Pillows were arranged around his body and appeared to be supporting his skeletal frame. Barrossa's once full head of hair was gone. Gray wisps clung to his nearly bald scalp. When he got closer Loyal could see the blue streaks of veins tracking across Barrossa'a head. The man was hooked up to a hospital grade monitor that was keeping track of his pulse, temperature, and heart rate. A blood pressure cuff was attached to the monitor as well. A tube snaked from an oxygen canister, alongside the bed, and up past Barrossa's chin into his nostrils.

The nurse stood beside Barrossa's bed. Her arms were crossed in front of her and she was glaring at Loyal with undisguised anger. Barrossa spoke first. His voice was quiet and he took long breaths of oxygen between each word.

"Leave us alone Audrey," he said.

She walked past Loyal and out the bedroom door. Loyal inched closer to the bed. His eyes locked onto Barrossa's and held. Neither man said anything for a long moment. Loyal broke the silence.

"My father kept a journal," he said.

"Where did you find it?" asked Barrossa in his slow painful way of speaking.

"Does it matter?" asked Loyal.

Barrossa shook his head slowly. "Suppose not," he said.

"The debt wasn't my father's," said Loyal. "My uncle had already paid with his life."

"Your father was smart," said Barrossa, "and brave. I never thought he'd run."

"You sponsored me to try to find him," said Loyal.

Barrossa nodded. "At first." He paused to inhale some oxygen. "It became clear quickly that you and your mother didn't know where he was."

"Then why continue?" asked Loyal.

Barrossa shrugged his frail shoulders. "You were a good kid," he said, "I liked you."

The men were silent for nearly a minute. The beeps from the monitor and Barrossa's hungry inhalations were the only sound. Finally Barrossa said, "You here to kill me?"

Loyal picked up one of the pillows from the bed and moved closer to Barrossa. An image formed in his mind of him pressing the pillow over the old man's face. He wouldn't last long. This image was quickly replaced by images of Stella,

Mason, and Trinity. He couldn't kill Barrossa. They wouldn't want him to. Loyal was surprised to hear a short laugh come out of his mouth. "I wanted to," he said, "but I like the idea of letting you stay alive and suffering." He tossed the pillow back on the bed. "You know where he got the money for my uncle?"

Barrossa nodded.

"Where?" asked Loyal.

Barrossa smiled. "Does it matter?" he asked.

The bedroom door opened and the nurse stepped into the bedroom.

"Your five minutes are up," she said as she pushed past Loyal and started fussing with Barrossa's blankets and pillows. Loyal turned and started towards the door. He paused when he reached the frame and turned back toward Barrossa.

"You hear from Tony lately?" he asked.

Barrossa shook his head.

"Huh," said Loyal, "I'd have thought he would have called. Last I heard he was in Holy Cross Hospital in Taos. Son of a bitch got himself shot."

Barrossa's eyes widened and the monitor started beeping loudly. Loyal simply turned and walked away.

117

LOYAL TRUESDALE

In the short time that Loyal had been inside Marco Barrossa'a residence the rain's intensity had increased dramatically. Fat drops, propelled by an angry wind, stung Loyal's face as he jogged to his truck. He slid in and quickly closed the door. As he reached to start the ignition he noticed a slight tremor in his hands. He flashed back to the moment in Barrossa's bedroom when he had stood by the old man's bed holding the pillow in his hands. He was certain he would have murdered the man if images of his loved ones had not slipped into his mind. He pushed this thought into a corner of his mind. Perhaps he would take it out later for examination. He wondered if his parting remark to Marco Barrossa had pushed the frail man closer to the brink, and decided that he didn't really care.

Loyal drove toward the gate and was relieved when it opened easily. He turned left on El Camino Real, then right onto Linea del Cielo and headed west toward the Coast Highway. He had just passed below Interstate 5 when his phone rang. It was connected to the truck through blue tooth so the caller's name showed on the truck's screen; Trinity. Loyal made a quick left and turned into the parking lot of Solana Beach Presbyterian Church. He parked then answered.

"Trinity," he said, "thank God."

"I'm not calling about us Loyal," she said.

"I found his journal Trinity," Loyal said, "I know everything now."

"Did he say anything about the money?" Trinity asked.

"It doesn't matter Trinity," he said, "I have closure now."

Trinity was quiet for a moment then said, "I never said we are done forever Loyal. We just need a break." She paused briefly then added, "We both do."

Loyal and Trinity were both quiet for a short time. Trinity broke the silence by saying, "I have something to tell you Loyal. It is about the money from the storage unit. I took a stack of twenties and had them analyzed."

Loyal heard her take a long breath in and slowly let it out.

"I hope you are sitting down Loyal," she said, "because you are not going to believe this."

118

WALKER TRUESDALE - NOVEMBER 24, 1971

After Walker had dropped Jameson at the bed and breakfast he had driven to Lake Merwin, Washington and parked his truck in some dense brush off the road about a mile south of the lake. Dressed in a black suit and carrying a black attache case, he had started walking along the road with his thumb out. Twenty minutes after he had begun hitchhiking he had been picked up by an older man driving a battered pale blue 1960 Ford F-100. He had pulled up next to Walker and asked where he was headed.

"Portland," Walker had told him.

"I can get you as far as Woodland," the man had said. "You can probably find a ride south on I 5 from there pretty easily." A hound dog had been sitting in the front passenger seat. "You'll have to hop in the bed," the man had said, "Buster here ain't giving up his seat."

Walker had hopped into the bed of the truck and settled himself up against the cab. The day had been cold and the suit he had been wearing had offered little protection from the frigid wind. He had pushed all thoughts of his plan to get the money for Jameson out of his mind and focused on Rita and Loyal instead. The drive to Woodland had taken just over half an hour. The driver had dropped Walker off in front of America's Family Diner on N Goerig Street. Walker had welcomed the warmth of the diner as he had entered. He had stayed long enough to drink two cups of coffee and eat a piece of cherry pie. He had walked the three blocks from the diner to the freeway on-ramp, picked a spot to stand, and had once again stuck out his thumb.

His ride this time had come in the form of a bright red 1970 Ford Mustang. The driver, who had introduced himself as Bobby Edwards, had been a young man in his twenties. He had worn blue jeans and a black leather jacket, had shoulder length brown hair, and had sported a bushy mustache. Bobby had been a talker, which Walker had appreciated. He had sat in the passenger seat and listened to Bobby's stories while they sped south to Portland. When Walker had asked, Bobby had recommended the Heathman Hotel on SW Broadway. He had dropped Walker there just over half an hour after he had picked him up in Woodland. Walker had spent Monday, Tuesday, and Wednesday at the Heathman. He had paid cash for the room and only left it to eat.

On Thursday, November 24, he checked out of the hotel and took a taxi to Portland International Airport. He purchased a ticket from Northwest Orient Airline on flight 305 which was traveling to Seattle. He paid cash for the ticket and gave his name as Dan Cooper. When he boarded he chose the middle seat in the back row on the right. He placed the attache case on is lap and ordered a bourbon and soda. When the stewardess strapped herself into the jump seat across from him in preparation for takeoff he handed her a folded note which she placed in her pocket unopened. He leaned toward her and said, "Miss, you'd better look at that note. I have a bomb."

AFTERWORD

The story of Dan (D.B.) Cooper has been a source of fascination for me my entire life. I have always held out hope that he survived the jump from the plane and escaped the densely wooded terrain into which he would have landed. Perhaps he returned to whatever life he had been living prior to November 24, 1971 and slowly spent the cash over a lifetime. If you happen to find a twenty dollar bill from 1969 you can run the serial number through Check-six.com, D.B. Cooper's serial number loot tracker, and see if you might be holding a piece of history.

ACKNOWLEDGMENTS

A woman approached me in a public place and said, "You are Kathleen Helms. I've read your books." Her comment gave me the goose bumps. It means so much to me when people tell me they enjoyed the books. So my first thank you goes to you, the reader, for taking the time to read this book. I'm incredibly grateful.

As always, I am indebted to my cold readers: Terry Coker, Madison and Edith Cooper, Hayley Helms, and Mark Palmerton. Your ability to honestly share your thoughts and concerns helps make each book the best that it can be.

Gratitude, again, to Detective Terry Coker, LASD (ret.) who patiently answered all my questions regarding police work and guns. Any errors in that regard are mine alone.

My deepest appreciation to Marta Palmerton, Mother and dear friend, for editing the proof and for believing in me.

A big thank you to Kym McNabb for another captivating cover and the perfect tweaking of the blurb on the back of the book.

Cheers to Hannah LaVine who always buys one of the first copies, reads, and share her thoughts with me.

To Brett, who I adore, goes my deepest appreciation of all. He brainstorms, listens, suggests, and holds my hand through the entire process. I love you Brett.

ALSO BY KATHLEEN HELMS

A.I. Smith

Loyalty

Mistrust

All are available on Amazon.com